CUT BACK
TO LIFE

MIRANDA
ARMSTADT

ACKNOWLEDGMENTS

As a first-time novelist, I was blessed with the incredible support of Doug Duke. Because of your unwavering and ever-patient mentoring from start to finish of this book—and the 10,000 questions you answered for months about every aspect of the self-publishing process—I was able to move ahead at lightning speed. I could not have done this without you. Thank you from the bottom of my heart.

To neurosurgeons everywhere—who put the broken back together every day with their incredible skills—thank you for your amazing dedication and abilities. I have experienced first-hand the metamorphosis your magic creates, and will always remain indebted for the new shot at life it has given me.

Damonza.com has been a wonderful design firm to work with to create my cover design and book formatting. Thank you for bringing my vision to life with your amazing cover and copy graphics, and for your patience throughout the formatting process.

"… sometimes you have to slice down to the bone to rebuild your soul…"

PREFACE

When I found out I would need spinal surgery, I was shocked, to say the least. I was told by my surgeon that without it, I would be in for ever-increasing pain and possible partial paralysis. Feeling I had no choice, I moved ahead.

The recovery journey was not an easy road, nor was it always smooth. But the lessons I took away about facing pain head-on and allowing healing to happen in its own time (and its imperfect processes), have transformed my life in so many ways.

The year of my surgery turned out to be one of complete metamorphosis. It is hard to put into words, even for a writer, the many aspects that unfolded for me beyond just freeing me from the harrowing pain I suffered from before my spinal fusion. One of them was the idea for this book.

I hope the characters in "Cut Back to Life" and their fictional journey will speak to anyone who has suffered physically or emotionally, and at times even given up hope of ever finding peace. Miracles do happen, even among mere mortal men.

I will never be the same.

Miranda Armstadt
November 2019

CHAPTER ONE

THE FIRST CUT IS THE DEEPEST

ANNA PORTER LAY spread-eagled, face down on the operating table, her limbs secured so tautly that she couldn't move even a fraction of an inch. Surrounded by men and women in head-to-toe medical garb that obscured all but their eyes, she had been rendered unconscious by the anesthesiologist and would soon be cut down to the bone on her lower back, just above her ass.

She'd had to bow out of her latest movie project—one her agent had pushed hard to land for the stunning 63-year-old star—when nerve pain in her right leg became so overwhelming that she was in tears on half of any given day. Now the film was on hold until Porter was good to go again, assuming she ever would be. She had two months, she'd been told by the producers, to come back to work, or she'd be replaced, per a stipulation in her contract.

Anna knew it was a do-or-die moment in her nearly 50-year movie career. If she lost this part, it was unlikely that she could ever recover her momentum, and she wasn't ready to give up stardom—and the material benefits that came with it—just yet.

But her sciatic nerve was being crushed by her cracked L5 vertebra, her celebrity neurosurgeon Dr. Mark Scofield told her, causing the extreme pain and likely to bring on even more if she didn't have surgery immediately. The micro-fracture was the result of an unusual genetic predisposition, and its instability had pushed the bottom vertebra on her spine almost off of its sacral base.

More critically, if she continued to crush the key nerve, Scofield told Porter, she could lose most of the function in her right foot, become incontinent, and even lose her ability to orgasm, realities that had forced her to put the operation ahead of her lucrative movie project.

Scofield—one of L.A.'s most renowned and accomplished neurosurgeons—stood poised between her parted legs and surveyed the carnage. For a man with nearly 30 years' experience in one of medicine's most demanding and difficult fields, he was taken aback by how much worse Anna's L5 and sacrum looked than even her MRI had indicated. He started to sweat, a condition that was unfamiliar to the normally calm, cool and extremely self-confident spine surgeon to Los Angeles' most elite inhabitants.

He'd performed more than 20,000 such spine surgeries over the course of his 28 years in private practice in Santa Monica and his eight years' prior residency at Johns Hopkins. Not much shook him up anymore. But looking at Anna's cracked vertebra and oddly curved sacrum, he knew this wasn't going to be an easy surgery.

He had mastered and even developed techniques to the point where the typically three-to-four-hour procedure was reduced to just over an hour in his practiced hands, but with three more surgeries to perform that day after Anna's, he told a nurse to let administration know those operations would be starting late.

Very late, it turned out.

As Dr. Scofield leaned over Anna's exposed spine, sinewy separated muscles, and slender core—medical power drill in hand—he felt something he hadn't felt in a very long time: trepidation. The unusual angle of her sacrum and the crack in her L5 meant he had but one chance to place the four-inch titanium screws correctly, to allow for a spinal fusion between the bottom vertebra and the bone plate between her hips to form over the next year or so.

But the drill and screws had to go through a gauntlet of nerves and nerve endings without hitting a single one. If he got it wrong, she could be paralyzed forever.

He was used to being revered for his surgical prowess, but suddenly felt like an intern again, with that rush of fear he recalled from the first time he had held a drill on an actual, living patient, not a cadaver.

Beads of sweat gathered on Scofield's forehead and started to pour down his armpits and through his surgical gown as he considered the point of attack. If he got it wrong, Porter's vertebra could split in half, which would not only be a disaster for her, but for his prestigious career as well. He had testified as an expert witness at many medical malpractice lawsuits, and suddenly envisioned being the defendant in one instead. The sweat continued to pour to the point where his assistant brought over a fresh gown and changed it for him, wiping his forehead as well.

"Get a grip on yourself," the doctor thought in his own head. Like a ravine that had to be jumped as if his very life depended on its successful crossing, he gathered his focus. He didn't have to tell anyone in the OR not to so much as breathe while he determined where the drill needed to be positioned for the four screws and accompanying rods to land correctly.

Suddenly, he was back in his expert mode, a master of his trade. No one else existed around him as he pressed the power button and pushed the first screw through Porter's delicate bones.

An audible sigh of relief could be heard from everyone around him as his assistant wiped more sweat from Scofield's brow.

"If that had been my first surgery – and not my 23,000[th] – it would have been my last," he whispered to Paul Crawford, his trusted physician's assistant of 18 years. Paul nodded solemnly in agreement. Having been in the OR with his boss many thousands of times, he knew that cases like Anna's might show up once every five years, if that. He knew, too, how easily these cases could end in disaster in the hands of anyone less capable than his revered boss.

Crawford closed the star's three-inch-long incision like a plastic surgeon, knowing how large a role vanity played in the lives of Hollywood's top players. He placed a large drain next to it to catch the inevitable bloody fluid that would be pouring out for the next 24 hours at least.

After slowly and carefully wrapping her wound, the medical team turned Porter back over and gently lay her on the hospital bed that would be wheeled first into recovery and then to her private room at UCLA Medical Center in Santa Monica. The anesthesiologist carefully de-intubated her and brought the actress out of her deep drug-induced coma. Medical staff then wheeled the groggy star into recovery, where she slept deeply for two hours.

CHAPTER TWO

TRAINER TO THE STARS

ROGER NILES—ANNA PORTER'S British boyfriend and personal trainer of just over a year—stood over her hospital bed in the spacious private room she was transferred to from recovery. He was annoyed to have had to reschedule several celebrity training appointments due to the long round-trip commute at rush hour in L.A.'s notoriously horrendous traffic.

Chiseled and tan, Niles seldom wore shirts during his typical work days, and felt almost uncomfortable when fully dressed and unable to showcase his nearly perfect and ripped physique. He'd built a following by being both ruggedly handsome—with just the slightest stubble growth to give him a rougher look in a city filled with manbuns—and by being brutally tough on his clients, who were 95 percent female and whose livelihoods depended on being as close to physically ideal as human beings can be.

He knew from experience that most of these women were insecure. While they may have been used to adoration from their legions of social media fans, on a more personal level, most had had absent or abusive fathers and felt more comfortable with a man who berated them frequently. Roger Niles didn't disappoint on that front, and it came naturally to him to do so.

When he and Anna had taken their trainer-client relationship to a more personal level, it was right after a particularly hard session that had reduced her to tears. Niles moved into comfort mode with a hug and a caress of her long, luxurious auburn hair, and one thing led to another, which in L.A. is as normal as a chai latte with almond milk at the Starbucks drive-through on any given morning at 6 a.m.

In the movie business, the blurry lines between professional interactions and personal ones are crossed so frequently that no one really knows where those lines are or what they look like, anyway.

Niles made a healthy living, charging $150 an hour to his workout clients. But Anna's fame and red-carpet appearances were something he relished being associated with, not to mention the free advertising it offered him when he showed up by her side on E! or TMZ.

Looking down at her, now awake, in the hospital bed, with no makeup on and her hair flowing on the white sheets as if she were a mermaid underwater, he thought how naturally beautiful she truly was, despite being close to two decades older than he was. Niles had learned young to manipulate women of all ages, but Anna held her own better than most, providing a slight challenge for the jaded and cynical Brit.

Roger liked his life uncomplicated, which was another reason he'd been attracted to Anna with her 17 years of seniority on him. In Hollywood, 63 isn't like it is anywhere else, so physically, she could easily pass for being in her early forties, meaning he had no trouble getting it up for her in the sack without the aid of Viagra. And she was no more in love with him than he was with her, a reality that worked well for both of them.

Training and sex constituted the majority of their interactions. Niles was no intellectual, although he possessed street smarts in spades. Anna had almost no formal education herself, but she, too, knew her way around from hard-earned experience, and many decades of it to boot.

Years of small plastic surgery fixes, fillers and Botox—along with her rigorous workouts—had kept her relatively ageless, and even stripped of good lighting and makeup, her natural beauty, high cheekbones, and large green eyes were striking.

"Hey baby," she said smiling hazily, unable to reach out to him with both hands still completely needled up and overflowing with a variety of labels, drains, and IV fluids. She was catheterized and had not yet been cleared to walk. She was also still pleasantly high on the massive cocktail of anesthesia, nerve blocks, Oxycodone, and lack of any solid food for the past 24 hours.

Porter smiled the smile of the chemically buzzed: a grin about nothing but having all of her pain completely shut down for the short-term.

"Hey," Roger said, touching the tips of her perfectly gel-manicured fingers, the only part of her body not directly hooked up to something, save the pulse oximetry monitor on her right index digit.

"You did good," he said, presenting the perfectly practiced expression of a man who knows how easily he can get a woman to jump into bed with him. "You need to rest. Doc said you can't eat anything solid for a day, but the nurses can bring you sugar-free popsicles and pudding if you're hungry."

But Anna had already drifted back to sleep, the sly smirk still evident on her face. Roger placed her hand back on the sheet and walked out of the hospital room, hoping to make it home before rush hour turned into a full-fledged parking lot from Santa Monica back to Malibu.

⌖

Anna was awake the next day when Scofield and his P.A. Paul Crawford did their rounds. It was a non-surgery day for the doctor, and he was dressed in a crisply starched white shirt, conservative tie, and grey suit slacks: his non-operating uniform.

His clean-shaven face and classic good looks—along with his 6' 3" very fit physique—had caught Anna's attention (along with most of his female patients over the years) and his calm and patient demeanor during their pre-op MRI review meetings had spurred something of a crush on her part. Crawford had even told her how brilliant the doctor was, and she was struck that someone who worked so closely with Scofield still held him in such high esteem after such a lengthy partnership.

She'd had every good-looking man she'd ever wanted, but Scofield was in a different category that left her feeling less confident in her ability to attract him. And now he'd seen her face down, scrubbed with surgical iodine's bizarre deep orange tint, with a catheter up her vagina and a tube down her throat, on a table where she'd been strapped in like a Mafia canary about to get tortured with a buzz saw.

She'd sensed in her pre-op office visits just the hint of some physical attraction from the doctor towards her—and she certainly felt it strongly towards him—but he was so professional and unreadable that her normal cues for such things didn't seem entirely reliable.

Anna knew from things Crawford had told her that the doctor was recently divorced and had two grown kids in their twenties. And while that meant there might be a window of entry for her, he was likely reeling after doling out millions in alimony settlements after ending his 20-year marriage.

Unlike with Niles—where their relationship was uncomplicated and potentially easily severable on either side—Anna sensed that any involvement with the neurosurgeon would be quite the opposite, if it ever got off the ground at all. But for someone like the star, who had high anxiety behind the façade of perfection she showed the world, his grounded confidence kept drawing her back in.

And now he was towering over her bedside, checking vitals with Paul and looking earnestly at her wound, which happened to hover directly above her delicately perfect—and now totally uncovered—derrière.

"Not sure if we're letting you out today," Scofield said quietly as he continued looking her over. He picked up her blood-infused wound drain and put it back down. "This needs to slow down before we can release you."

He closed her gown and stood back a few inches from her bed.

Anna—still fairly high from intravenous pain meds and the residual effects of anesthesia—smiled charmingly at him, less self-conscious than she would have been otherwise to let him see her with no makeup and dressed in two less-than-fashionable overlapping hospital gowns and bright yellow socks with rubber treads that had been put on her feet to keep her from slipping once she started walking.

She had a nasal cannula invisibly delivering oxygen to her and leg pumps that kept her circulation going to prevent embolisms from forming in her calves.

"Whatever you say, doc," she said, and would have grabbed his hand if either of hers had been less burdened with hospital paraphernalia. Her perfect, professionally whitened teeth and natural dimples were all she had to work with in this situation, along with her innate charisma that had enchanted dozens of men before the doctor entered the picture.

He remained unflappable and smiled in that way that left her unsure if it was a professional mannerism or a silent chuckle to her high-ness. "Paul will check on you again in an hour or two," Scofield said, and left the room.

Anna felt a twinge that she hadn't since she was 10 and lovestruck by Steve McQueen when the original "Thomas Crown Affair" came out in 1966. And Scofield seemed equally unattainable to her. He was undoubtedly still raw from his divorce and probably dating 27-year-olds, she thought. He certainly would have no problem attracting whoever he set his sights on, she knew that much. He was pushing 60, but that was no detriment to a man in a town that was fueled by money and power in men and beauty and youth in women.

And he certainly wasn't hard on the eyes.

But while Scofield operated on Hollywood stars, he wasn't "in" Hollywood the way that most of her social circle—not to mention her last six boyfriends—had been. He moved in more intellectually elite company, and was likely less moved by beauty after so many years of practicing in Santa Monica, where good looks are almost ho-hum.

Anna closed her eyes and drifted back to sleep, dreaming of the doctor picking her up in the way that Clark Gable scooped up Scarlett in "Gone with the Wind," carrying her upstairs to have his way with her.

CHAPTER THREE

SHAKEN, STIRRED AND AROUSED

MARK SCOFIELD, MD, FACS returned to his 2,800-square-foot, $4.5 million Santa Monica home the night he did Anna's surgery more shaken than even when his wife faced off with him in his lawyer's office during their divorce. Despite having successfully completed the star's complex spinal fusion and laminectomy, he felt oddly off-balance, as if he'd had one too many cocktails and been asked to walk a straight line by a CHP officer immediately after.

It had been almost a year since his divorce had been finalized, and although Scofield had gone on a date here or there when traveling out of state for medical conventions, he hadn't slept with a single one of the very attractive—and all much younger—women he'd wined and dined. He knew he could have sex with any of them with little effort, and even more easily simply by dropping the "MD" into dinner conversation early on. But it just wasn't what he was about, and never had been, despite his good looks and success.

Scofield's prominence in neurosurgery was something he'd

been groomed for since childhood. It was like a construction trade for really, really smart, incredibly educated over-achievers who liked the rush of holding someone's mobility in their hands.

As Scofield had been reminded earlier that day, whether or not you could hit your target with a bullseye was key in neurosurgery and there was never room for error, as every surgeon's malpractice insurance in this specialty could attest. He had started to sweat just thinking about it driving home in his late-model silver Porsche 911 Carrera S, an atypically flashy car that he'd paid $123,000 for after the divorce was finalized to distract and reward himself for getting through it.

Focus had never been a problem for the doctor: not now, and not growing up, either. In his Midwestern Episcopalian home in Ohio, he'd learned to compete in athletics under duress, and had always been at the top of his class, easily getting into Harvard as an undergraduate and then into its medical school with his near-perfect MCAT score of 528 and his GPA of 3.98. He was unrelenting in his study habits and was accepted into Johns Hopkins in Baltimore—one of the top three hospitals in the country from a prestige standpoint—for his neurological surgery internship and residency after graduation.

His ex-wife—a local Baltimore girl-next-door type whom he'd met during those early years and who was initially excited to be a neurosurgeon's wife—grew tired after almost two-and-a-half decades of having to do everything to keep the house running and raise their two now-grown kids, and found her way into the arms of a lawyer with better hours and fewer life-and-death decisions to consider several times a week, ones that had kept Scofield away from home well into the evening on many a work day.

They had waited a few years after marrying to have children—until his L.A. practice was solid and his reputation secure—so his oldest, a boy, was now 22 and his youngest, a daughter, 20. The girl was at Pepperdine pursuing a liberal arts degree and the right social connections to marry well, and his son had just graduated from his father's alma mater and was in his first year of law school at Yale. He saw them mostly just on holidays now, events which were painfully tense and uncomfortable for everyone and which he had already come to dread.

He'd missed a lot of their childhood and adolescence while he worked, and was now paying the price for that by having a relationship with each of them that largely involved sending them money.

The doctor pulled the Carrera into his three-car garage and went inside to the deafening silence of his perfectly decorated, uber-modern home. He'd hired a pro to pick out everything for him after the divorce, unable to focus on so many design details between surgeries and office visits with patients. The elegant home was muted in tone, to provide a relaxing sense of visual white noise at the end of his long, stressful days.

Scofield never did two surgery days in a row, so he poured himself a glass of Scotch on the rocks and sank into the café-mocha-colored velveteen sofa and sighed. Today's surgery had thrown his equilibrium so far off kilter that he hadn't yet regained it, and he wasn't used to feeling so out of control emotionally. He took a few sips of whiskey and suddenly started to sob violently, crying so loudly his neighbors would have heard him if he'd had any that were closer than 100 feet away.

But the emotional outburst didn't last long. An expert at self-control, the doctor grabbed tissues from the marbled guest half-bathroom just steps from the sofa and blew his nose hard, wiped it, tossed the tissues in the trash, and threw back the rest of his drink rapidly. Then he rinsed the glass in the sink and left it on the counter for his twice-weekly cleaning lady to deal with.

Scofield loosened his tie and unbuttoned his shirt, revealing the same firm chest and abs he'd had since his high school days, even though he was now 59 years old and looking down the barrel of 60 in just a few weeks. As with everything else in his life, he was disciplined about what he ate, and worked out at least twice a week at the gym, plus running distance on weekends.

He looked at himself in his full-length bedroom mirror and felt content with the totally naked image staring back at him. No extra fat, no man boobs, no mid-life belly. His body was exactly like his brain: finely tuned and perfectly calibrated on all fronts.

The doctor always slept in the nude, as pajamas and t-shirts in bed bothered him. He suddenly saw Anna's makeup-less face smiling facilely up at him from her hospital bed, and felt a warm shiver come over him. He couldn't deny that he'd been struck by her beauty the first time she'd come into his office with her MRIs, complaining of extreme pain in her right leg. And, of course, he recognized her from her many leading movie roles over the years.

He'd never been one to be impressed with anyone from Hollywood. His upbringing had encompassed none of that, and L.A.'s beauty culture didn't resonate in any deep way with him. His ex-wife—whom he'd met when they were both in their early 20s—had evolved into a Neiman-Marcus, SoCal Stepford wife, but not at all at his behest. In fact, he disliked lots of makeup on women, and found Anna most striking lying in that hospital bed bare-faced and uncontrived.

He smiled thinking about her, even as he shook his head at how terrifyingly close to disaster her surgery could have been earlier that day. He suddenly felt an erection coming on, and got into bed so he could take care of it. He hadn't had any actual sex in well over a year since his divorce, and not much for at least two years before it all ended. So self-pleasuring had become almost mechanical, as just a way to keep his hormones from running amok. He washed himself with a wet cloth afterwards, and fell asleep still thinking about Anna Porter.

CHAPTER FOUR

THE FUSE IS LIT

SCOFIELD WOKE EARLIER than usual the next day, and felt re-established in his own mind as L.A.'s pre-eminent neurosurgeon. He called Crawford to coordinate their rounds at the hospital, and checked in with his service to see how many appointments he had at his office later that afternoon. Spines were a lot like plumbing: you could count on so many of them to have chronic issues at any given time, it was always a safe bet that he would never run out of potential new patients.

He made black coffee and slid into the Porsche to head back towards the hospital. As the sleek sports car picked up speed and he shifted gears, he felt his own heart beating a bit faster at the thought of seeing Anna again, bare-faced and bare-assed. He unconsciously felt the sensation of running his hands down her lower back when she'd first come to see him, and how he'd thought how perfect her alabaster, un-sun damaged skin was. Clearly, this wasn't someone who'd lain out on the Santa Monica beaches and sunbathed in their youth.

But when he felt another erection start, he mentally splashed cold water on himself and gulped back more coffee at the final stop light before the hospital.

Just as in the OR the day before, he told himself to get his shit together. He pulled up to the hospital valet and turned over his keys to the skinny, uniformed boy who knew the doctor's car from a block away. "See you at noon, Dr. Scofield," the kid said, and jumped into a car that could only be a fantasy for him for decades to come, moving it into gear.

The doctor walked slowly into the hospital lobby and found Paul Crawford waiting for him already. They were as familiar with each other's patterns as an old married couple after 18 years of working together, and headed towards the elevator to start rounds.

Anna was third on the list. She was eating a popsicle when he came in and looked almost childlike with a bright orange tongue and that grin he found irresistible. He put on his "serious doctor" face that he'd mastered during his residency years and approached her with Paul, who picked up her drain.

"Still pretty full of fluid, we'll keep you one more night to be safe," Scofield said, looking overly stern as he spoke to Anna to avoid betraying the slightly giddy feeling he had being in her presence.

"Have you gotten out of bed and walked yet?" he asked, noting that the intermittent pneumatic compression devices had now been removed from her legs and the catheter pulled as well.

"I have," she said, sucking the popsicle in a way that he sensed was entirely to taunt him. She still looked groggy, though, and her hair by now was totally disheveled. The doctor wanted to run his fingers through it, but instead, stuffed his hands awkwardly into his pants pockets. Even Crawford noticed the move and grinned quizzically at the doc, as he'd never seen him do that in all their years together.

"That was a really difficult surgery," Scofield said, looking down at her. "You scared us a little."

"Really?" Anna replied, suddenly waking up a bit and pushing herself slightly higher in the hospital bed. Any movie star is their own favorite topic of conversation, and Anna was no different. "Like, on a scale of 1 to 10, how hard was it?" she said suggestively.

"10," Mark said, without missing a beat or the double-entendre, and Crawford laughed. He couldn't remember the last time he'd seen his boss sweat like he had in the OR the day before, not even at a charity tennis match in Beverly Hills, surrounded by uber-hot 20-something models and actresses in short tennis skirts and too-tight buttoned-down cotton shirts.

"You made me rethink my choice of profession for a moment," Scofield said, looking earnestly into Anna's green pools for eyes, hoping to verify interest on her part, even though he knew it was an utterly ridiculous scenario.

It wasn't like he could possibly date her, even if she was interested in him. It would break every medical code of ethics and set himself up for potential liability, or even having his license to practice pulled by the State Board. It was a situation he'd assiduously avoided over decades of practice, even when he'd been approached by leggy young Hollywood actresses who would have given him a blow job right in his office.

It just wasn't worth the risk.

Was it?

CHAPTER FIVE

PICKING UP THE PIECES

ROGER NILES CAME to the hospital the next day to bring Anna Porter home. Dr. Scofield had surgeries at another location, so an in-house doctor on the orthopedic ward had checked the actress's drains, found the fluids to be receding satisfactorily, and signed her release form.

A nurse brought a wheelchair in and Roger lifted her out of bed and set her down in it. She was still on enough narcotics that nothing hurt too badly.

The ride down in the elevator was silent. The valet brought the personal trainer's Land Rover around and again, Roger's taut and muscular biceps easily lifted Anna into the front seat of the SUV. She strapped herself in, wincing a bit as she moved. She was wearing the yoga pants and loose cotton T-shirt she'd worn in on surgery day, had no makeup on, and didn't really care how she looked or that she hadn't brushed her teeth that morning. It wasn't like they were going to go home to get it on, after all.

Niles had seen her day in, day out, sweating and

makeup-less, while wearing grungy workout gear. She'd never felt any need to impress him, because on that level, she truly didn't care that much what he thought about her. Roger and Anna's relationship was mechanical and lacked emotion, as neither was actually in love with the other.

For Anna, Roger was convenient: she had her trainer right there before dawn to get her workouts in before she had to be on movie sets at 5 a.m. for hair and makeup. She knew she lacked the motivation to add a 45-minute roundtrip drive to that equation, and staying in shape—at her age especially—was quintessential to her career continuing. At 5' 5" and 118 pounds, Anna was only three pounds heavier now than she had been at 20, but it wasn't getting any easier to stay that way.

She had always drawn men to her delicate frame, exuding something incredibly fragile that might break, like a piece of fine china, if they went too far. Men liked pushing the envelope there, seeing how hard they could fuck her without actually breaking a bone. Anna accepted it as part of the Hollywood system as well as just how men are, and used it to her advantage, since there was no escaping it anyway.

For Mark Scofield—himself consumed by some of these thoughts—it was actually good to have a reason not to come see Anna again that morning before she checked out of the hospital. He needed to block her out of his lusty mind completely, he had decided, and out of sight seemed like a good place to start.

He hadn't felt this erotically charged by any other woman in his entire life, and it was driving him mad. Used to having complete control of his emotions, focus, and brain—habits drilled into him from childhood by his college professor father, and throughout medical school and his residency at Johns Hopkins—Scofield was annoyed that Anna had somehow gotten around all of his carefully managed stop gaps and now popped up in his mind constantly, consequently causing his dick to pop up at sometimes inopportune moments where he would have to hide it or turn away when in public.

He had thought about making love to her and he had thought about fucking her, but either way, he felt packed with powerful emotions that he didn't want to feel. He knew that everything about these sensations would backfire on him and thus, they were nothing but a burden. But he couldn't shake them, no matter how hard he tried.

He decided that when he saw her next—which would be when he examined her to see how she was healing after Crawford removed her staples at ten days—he would realize that it was all a figment of his imagination and complete silliness. In that sense, he almost looked forward to that day, so that he could just get on with it and forget about her. A neurosurgeon has no time for such an infatuation, he thought, and an attraction to a patient was completely, totally, unequivocally out of bounds for any doctor, let alone one of his stature.

He'd tried a rare weekend of golfing—a sport he mostly detested, finding it dull—and another of tennis, which he liked better. But neither activity, undertaken with medical colleagues and their wives, helped distract him in the slightest, much to his annoyance, and he would still go home and jerk off thinking about the petite actress obsessively.

⁂

Anna had fallen asleep as soon as Roger carried her into the bedroom when they got home from the hospital. He was happy to watch some sports in the huge living room of her Malibu beach front home and not have to tend to her, as nurturing was not in his skill sets. He prepared some blow and snorted a bit of cocaine, a habit that was becoming more frequent for him of late. It was easy to score in the high-end lifestyle to which he'd become accustomed, and he had plenty of money to buy it.

Plus, it gave him a high that made him feel invincible, a feeling he relished. Anna had, of course, seen him snorting the white powder, but being Hollywood, it wasn't anything she hadn't seen before. She'd been around chemically altered people since her earliest days, and while she herself never partook, it didn't seem out of the ordinary to her at all.

The surf crashed dramatically outside as the afternoon came and went, and Anna slept almost nonstop till the next morning. She dreamt that Dr. Scofield was yelling at her in his office, telling her he couldn't get involved with her and she should stop trying to seduce him. Little did she know how accurately the dream reflected the doctor's reality and his struggle to wrestle loose of her hold.

She woke up smiling, like the cat who ate the canary. She, too, looked forward to meeting again, but not with the same goal in mind as the doctor. On the contrary—coming from a profession with no HR departments and virtually no regulations about anyone's behavior on a set—the thought of doing the doctor was delicious to her, and had no downside whatsoever.

CHAPTER SIX

DISSECTING A HEART

SCOFIELD HAD PICKED neurosurgery as his medical career path, both because it was so demanding, and because it required so much precision. He prided himself on being able to zero in on whatever had to be done with such focus and clarity that he only saw the problem that had to be solved, and nothing else.

He had been brought up in a largely emotionally bereft and sexually puritan home. That upbringing worked perfectly when he was in doctor mode, because not betraying a single feeling or sexual impulse to patients came naturally to him.

But Anna had put a large crack in that façade and he wasn't happy about that fact one bit. At the same time, she made him feel giddy in a way that he hadn't since tenth grade, when he fell in love with his hot 32-year-old math teacher. That had been unrequited, at least in the real sense, although the teacher's image had come to bed with him every night in his own mind—and via his own hand as he went at it under the sheets when he knew his parents were asleep.

Somehow, he was back there now with Anna, relishing his fantasies of vanquishing her. But he was no longer 15 and gawky, and she was due in his office in eight days to get the staples removed from her back. Which meant seeing that perfect ass and exquisite face again. He worried that he might get an erection and was glad that at least Paul would remove the staples, and that he only had to speak to Anna after it was done and she was fully clothed.

But in his own fantasies at night, he would touch her wound repeatedly—which rested in the most sensual part of the human body, the lower back—and get massively hard thinking about doing so.

Mark wondered if Paul had noticed the sexual tension he felt around her, and guessed he had, but that he was too discreet to say anything.

In fact, Paul knew that Scofield was probably ripe for a dalliance at any moment, but had suspected it would be with one of the neurosurgeon's out-of-town, never-to-be-seen again dates, not with a major star who would be coming in for follow-ups for several months to come.

⁂

Back home in Santa Monica, Mark poured himself a Scotch and soda that night after surgery. The masturbation sessions had become so regular that he'd taken to changing his own sheets so that the cleaning lady wouldn't think he was having different girls over every night. The last thing he needed was any gossip spreading around town about him. He still hadn't gotten entirely comfortable with the idea that he was single and free to do whatever he wanted once more.

Scofield also overlooked the obvious reality that a relation-ship with a major Hollywood star would be tabloid fodder that would create a feeding frenzy of internet and social media photos. He'd never been exposed—as Anna had many times—to having people jump out of bushes or from behind trees to get a photograph that they could parlay into a nice payday for any of the major gossip rags.

All Dr. Mark Scofield knew was that it would be reckless beyond all consideration to contemplate taking up with Anna Porter on any level. And yet, it was all he could think about anymore, and almost like a drug addiction, he desperately wanted his fix.

He imagined taking her on the operating table, comatose and face down, as he pressed himself between her legs the way he had during her actual surgery. Only this time, he thrust his hard penis into her silky waiting pussy, and came all over the OR floor as the surgical techs watched.

Or playing with her clit under the table at an upscale Beverly Hills restaurant, while she responded by gently massaging his balls through the pants of a $2,500 suit.

Scofield pictured himself spanking her and then fucking her hard, as he softly touched her still-raw back wound and then came into it. In all of his fantasies, she climaxed slowly and let out a huge cry of pleasure as she came for what seemed like an eternity of ecstasy for both of them.

But far from giving him relief, the more the doctor fantasized, the worse his obsession became with Anna. He felt like he was spiraling out of control, rolling down a mountain on ice at breakneck speed, loving the rush, but terrified of the dead stop at the bottom and the broken bones—or hearts—that could ensue.

In his Ohio upbringing, where sex and love existed only in fantasy for him, his intense feelings on both fronts had been bottled up by force, as the slightest indication of either brought stern reprimands from his father. His stay-at-home mother acted like sex didn't even exist, and he sometimes wondered how he had come into the world between these two seemingly emotionless and extremely sexually repressed people.

His parents were both still alive back in his Ohio home-town, now in their mid-80s, and at an age where sex and romantic love were no longer much on the minds of any of their still-living contemporaries, making them appear less out-of-touch than they had when he was a boy.

As a child, he'd felt like a felon reading porn magazines with his school buddies in a rest room or at sleepovers, but the feelings had been so fantastic, he'd become stuck in a peren-nial cycle of sexual release and ecstasy followed by another of repression and shame.

There was no going back now, though, he realized: the cycle was only rotating in one direction, and it was delicious. Somehow, Anna had transformed him without even knowing him, and he knew he was going willingly towards a no-man's land of the most shunned practice in all of medicine: becoming romantically and sexually involved with a patient.

CHAPTER SEVEN

IN THE WAITING ROOM

B Y A WEEK later, when Anna came in to Scofield's office for her staple removal, she had fully re-embraced caring about her appearance. Somehow, she sensed that the doctor wasn't really a makeup guy, and used a light hand when applying it. She'd had her manicurist come to the house and do her nails the day before, but her toes were still too delicate to paint, as the pain had started to escalate post-surgically.

She'd pulled her hair up into a loose ponytail, with wispy strands falling around her face in a way that she knew from experience men found intoxicating. She couldn't wear anything tight around her bandage, so she threw on a soft, short sundress and lace panties, knowing the doctor would have to lift the dress to get to her back. She smiled thinking about it and shivered, imagining him wrapping his strong arms around her tiny waist and kissing her neck softly.

"Babe, let's go before the 1 becomes a parking lot," Roger bellowed at her from the kitchen in his Cockney accent, jingling car keys impatiently. He'd been in L.A. for 18 years and had never gotten used to the ubiquitous traffic congestion on every single road, including the coast highway.

Anna quickly changed her drenched panties to a fresh pair and hobbled out to the car. The tendons, muscles and ligaments that had been carefully pulled to each side of her exposed spine during surgery and held there with a metal frame for almost two hours were now screaming in agony, and her butt felt like she had climbed Mt. Everest backwards, twice. She popped another Oxycodone and some muscle relaxers and slowly climbed into the Land Rover, wincing as she did so, even with Roger's help.

In Scofield's waiting room, Anna was not the only L.A. notable. A celebrity defense attorney, a stunt man who she recognized from past films, and two other well-known actors all sat behind their dark sunglasses, intensely checking their cell phones and avoiding looking at anyone else.

The combination of pain and being slightly high from the pills made Anna less self-conscious than she would have normally been in the same situation. No one was looking at her anyway, not in this room full of industry types whose careers were all being put on hold while they underwent Scofield's recommended fixes.

She had waited almost an hour past her appointment time before a nurse called her into an exam room. After another 15 minutes passed, it was his P.A., Paul Crawford, who opened the door smiling, and Anna's disappointment was palpable.

Crawford was used to women having crushes on his boss, and to playing second fiddle to Scofield's rock star status. A physician's assistant to a top neurosurgeon cannot have a big ego and survive long in the gig, and Paul was perfectly suited to the task.

Anna now felt somewhat awkward about her choice of wardrobe, and wished she'd worn something with more cover.

She held up her dress as Crawford warned her it would sting a bit when he pulled the staples out. But the Oxy took the edge off and Anna—who hadn't eaten much since the surgery—felt slightly light-headed and woozy and barely noticed the staples coming out at all.

When he was done, Crawford wiped her wound down with Betadine and covered it with a light bandage just to keep it from oozing.

Anna sat down on a stool, feeling sexual and high from the drug.

"Stay put, Dr. Scofield will be in shortly to take a look and check how you're coming along," the P.A. said, standing up. "Nice to see you again, Miss Porter."

Crawford left her in the treatment room, her heart racing slightly with anticipation.

Scofield might as well have been her mirror in that regard: he hesitated when he pulled her chart out from the front door of the room and took a deep breath before entering. He had to push back a gasp when he saw her, she looked so delicate in that cotton sundress that he knew could only get him in trouble.

Normally, it would have annoyed him, but he felt a rush of happiness that he hadn't in a very long time seeing her. If he had been anywhere else, and hadn't known she was held together with nothing but titanium screws and rods for the moment, he might have picked her up and swirled her around in a rare moment of spontaneity. But Scofield's doctor manners were so well-ingrained that the thought was stuffed down quickly.

"Anna," he said warmly, extending a hand, as she quickly reached up and kissed him softly on the cheek, leaving him totally flustered. He blushed and laughed nervously. "How are you doing?" he asked, sitting down and pulling himself towards her on his rolling stool.

"Better now," she said, smiling sweetly and staring straight into his eyes in a way that made him feel naked to his core. He wanted to look away, but couldn't make himself. Instead, he pulled closer to her yet.

"Let's see how you're doing," he said. "Can I get you to stand for me?"

Stand she did, but he could tell she was unsteady on her feet, which forced him to hold her at the waist. It couldn't have been but 22 inches, and his large hands almost met coming around it. He asked her to pull up the cotton sundress and felt himself go beet-red in doing so, which she couldn't see as she was facing away from him so he could examine her back.

She held her dress and let him gently remove the gauze bandage. The wound brought up his sexual fantasies, which he had to hastily stuff back into the corners of his mind. His fingers perched around—but not on—the lesion, to keep it sterile, but the touch of her soft skin and the curve of her lower back was like some kind of lure designed to make sailors willingly drown to meet a mermaid.

Her ponytail flowed just to the nape of her neck, which he wanted to caress in the worst way possible. Instead, he wiped her incision down again with Betadine and placed a large bandage pad over the wound.

Then Anna turned around and looked at him, smiling so sensually that he almost couldn't breathe.

Towering over her, Scofield looked down into her eyes. He knew he couldn't fight it now, no matter if it cost him his career or everything he had ever worked for. The emotions, for once, were bigger than he was and he could not stave them off or push them away.

He leaned down gently and tipped her chin to his face to kiss her. She looked up at him like someone who has just gotten her way against all odds as their lips met. It felt like fire and ice and an earthquake all at once, a perfect storm in which they were both trapped willingly and more than happy to go wherever the typhoon took them.

He tenderly kissed her lips for as long as he dared, his eyes closed now, and then opened them feeling almost reborn. Maybe this was what love felt like, he thought suddenly, a thought he had never had before in his entire 59 years on Earth. Anna smiled at him like an angel and he felt like he had just returned with the spoils from war.

There was no point in addressing the inappropriateness of what had just happened in his own exam room, so he didn't. "I would love to see you sometime outside of a medical environment, if that's alright," Scofield said, with a confidence he had never felt before with any woman. Under the circumstances, that confidence made no sense, but nothing really did at that moment.

"Yes, we should," Anna almost whispered back, moving away and towards the door. "My boyfriend is waiting for me, but please, text me… soon."

"I'll walk you out," Scofield said, smiling back at her as he led her to the checkout desk, trying not to show the elation that filled his heart at that very moment.

CHAPTER EIGHT

CROSSING THE LINE

SCOFIELD WAS USED to dealing with partial information. In his line of work, there was no way to actually see what you were dealing with until you opened someone up, with MRIs and X-rays being all he had to go on before entering the OR and starting to slice and dice.

With an MRI, he could get a pretty clear look into what he would have to do, and how complex it might be. But sometimes, the way things read could be a tad misleading, confusing, or even confounding. Such had been the case with Anna's surgery. He hadn't expected it to be a 10 in difficulty from her imaging films, or even a 7 for that matter.

He wondered—as he poured his evening Scotch and plopped onto his sofa that night—if Anna herself were the same way: appearing to be relatively easy to read, but perhaps holding back some dark secret that he wouldn't discover until he was in way, way, way too deep, with no way to turn around and run.

But just as these occasional surgical realities hadn't stopped him from being a neurosurgeon, the doctor had no intention of not reaching into Anna's soul and seeing what showed up, no matter what it ultimately revealed. Even if it blew up on him. Which, he realized, it certainly could.

He was in a line of work where he cut people open, moved everything around, and then brought them back to life, piecing their broken spines together again. It was intense, and it was life-changing for his patients, and Scofield got a lot of satisfaction from knowing he had given them back their joy and their energy after what was often months—or even years—of suffering.

Mark Scofield, as a child—and even as a man—had seldom crossed any lines set by his demanding and strict father or his reserved and shut-down mother. But now he was about to do something that would inevitably become public, either via a revealing photograph or a hacked text or by Anna's boyfriend finding out and calling it in to police, or the Medical Board, or both.

He had never done anything so unequivocally reckless in his entire life, but he had no desire to turn back. For once, emotion had overridden reason for the doctor, and he found he rather liked the sensation.

He'd saved Anna's cell number into his phone from her office records, and was about to text her. She was still early in her recovery, with her real pain just starting and likely to continue for weeks, he knew. Should he wait until she was more on the mend? He should wait until never, he thought, chuckling, but that wasn't going to happen either, no matter how unadvised a game plan.

He pulled up his phone message function and entered her name, listed simply under "AP," and considered his approach. It felt almost as confusing as when he'd hovered over her open back with that surgical drill and tried to figure out how to get the screws and rods precisely where they needed to go.

In contrast to all the women he had wined and dined while traveling for business throughout the past year for medical conferences, Anna was an A-list movie star: used to Cannes, large yachts, and the glitz of Beverly Hills and Rodeo Drive. Maybe he needed something more novel and less predictable to win her over, he thought.

Besides, she wasn't going to be feeling well at all and couldn't drink while still on those pain meds.

He thought to himself that she could lie on the extremely soft and comfortable sofa and he could just hold her hand and stare into those emeralds she had for eyes.

After all, what did she care about how much money he spent on dinner, she didn't need a man to do that for her anyway. Comfort and care: that's what everyone wanted after surgery as they wept through the brutal pain of spasming muscles. If anyone knew that, it was the doctor who'd caused it thousands of times.

"Anna, it's Mark Scofield," he typed into the text box. "Wondering if I could bring you some TLC this weekend... Saturday, Sunday, both... you tell me." He wondered if it sounded slightly desperate.

But a smitten man has no pride, and he pressed "send."

◇

Anna hadn't expected to hear from Scofield so soon after their office kiss, and certainly not that same night. She didn't have his cell number in her contacts, so it was good he had said who it was at the top of the message.

Before she could get any further, he sent a follow up: "I'll send a luxury stretch limo and come with it, so you won't have to worry about anything."

The thought of the doctor pulling up in a limo was appealing indeed, but what was Anna to tell Roger? she wondered. Would he even care? Maybe they had run their course and he'd be glad to bail out now.

She knew she could figure that out. But she also knew she couldn't let Mark get her that easily. She had to give him some kind of challenge to meet, at least.

"Send a powder blue limo, and bring 300 tulips," she texted him back, laughing at her own silly and completely random request.

"Done," he replied. "Saturday at one o'clock?" He had not one clue where one found a powder blue limo, but this was L.A., and there had to be one somewhere he could order. The tulips were easy, albeit expensive, but what did he care?

"Make it 2 p.m., and bring soft slippers and a robe for me, too," she wrote, realizing she was so powerful with him right now, she could have requested a gilded carriage with four flying unicorns and he would have made it come together somehow.

"And I'm letting you off easy, cause I'm still hurting and high," she added.

Mark knew this was an absolute fact: that had she been in better shape or of sounder mind, this scenario would not have passed muster so easily. Timing is everything, he thought. He felt quite pleased with himself, and started Googling "blue limousines" immediately.

✑

Saturday couldn't come fast enough for Scofield. He hadn't been this excited about anything—let alone a woman—in decades. He struggled with what to wear and finally decided on jeans. And after all, he wore them well, his trim waist and firm stomach looking ruggedly handsome in them. He decided on a crisp white shirt to go with it, which he knew from experience was a bit of an aphrodisiac for many women. He imagined her ever-so-slowly unbuttoning it, too, and driving him right to the edge.

❧

As it turned out, Roger had plans to go out of town that weekend, something Anna hadn't even known about and that the trainer had forgotten to tell her: such was their lack of connection in even day-to-day life. He had a conference in Northern California with other trainers about the latest equipment and fitness trends, and in Hollywood, you had better be ahead of the curve in that regard. He was leaving on Friday and wouldn't return until Monday, he told her nonchalantly.

Perfect, Anna thought, breathing a sigh of relief, though she feigned some small degree of poutiness, so as not to show her hand.

❧

By the weekend and the day of her first date with Scofield, pain had hit her full throttle. Pulling anything over her head or even trying to stand on one leg to get on pants—let alone button anything around her now bandage-less waist—wasn't going to happen.

She couldn't do the sundress again without looking contrived, so she picked a button-down dress in white that unknowingly mirrored Mark's shirt.

Anna threw on cute flats and decided her tresses would fall loose this time, so that the doctor could get tangled up in all of it when he leaned in to kiss her.

At 1: 55 p.m., the ridiculous-looking Iowa prom-style powder blue limo pulled up into her driveway and Mark stepped out and rang her bell. The 300 tulips were already arranged all over his home: in various shades and exquisitely placed in 10 Waterford crystal vases by his favorite Santa Monica florist. He'd specified that he wanted the best of the best, and he got them: for almost five-thousand dollars, including the arrangements in his home and the high-end crystal display.

When Anna opened the door, his grin ran ear-to-ear as he held out his hand to help her down the steps to the driveway. He very carefully guided her into the car, which he'd made sure was full of soft but firm pillows to support her sore back and legs, and slid in next to her, forcing himself not to put his hand on her knee.

But Anna surprised him by quickly laying her head in his lap, almost startling him because he knew it would turn him on so much. The loose hair had the desired effect, as he immediately began stroking it and her soft and tiny neck, with his long, strong fingers. Anna sighed and smiled with her eyes closed dreamily as the doctor rolled up the window between them and the driver, even though he knew the guy could obviously see everything that was going on.

"You look exquisite," he said quietly, wanting to call her "baby," but thinking it would look presumptuous when they hadn't even been on a single date yet. Her eyes opened slightly and she smiled winsomely at him, then closed them again, like a child who feels secure in a soft bed.

"We'll get you comfortable at my house, don't worry," he continued, stroking her hair as if it were a champion Persian cat. "And I have the robe and slippers waiting, too. I didn't forget."

Much as he would have liked to have bought her something at Victoria's Secret, he knew she wanted comfort and that it would also have looked cocky to buy lingerie designed to come right off. Instead, he opted for a size two soft velvet short robe in lavender that he thought would look exquisite on her. It had been years since he had been in any stores that sold this kind of merchandise, and he'd forgotten how alluring it all was. He got her matching velvet slippers with boa feathers on them.

Everything was laid out for Anna on the sofa when they got to the house. She ooohed at all the tulips, amazed he had paid so much attention to detail—and paid so much, period. This afternoon, she knew, had cost him many thousands.

She turned to face him on the heavenly sofa, indicating with her searching eyes that it would be him doing the shirt unbuttoning of her white dress. He leaned down and started with the first button, shaking like a first-year intern doing an assist in surgery. She was wearing a soft cotton bra that showed enough of her perfect and petite breasts to arouse him instantly, and he knew there was no point in hiding it. With each button he opened, his erection grew until Anna reached over and slowly unzipped his jeans to caress his cock and then leaned over to take it into her mouth, even though it hurt her back to do so.

Mark stroked her hair and moaned, it had been so long since he had had these kinds of powerful sexual and emotional feelings. He felt like he was on morphine, only more awake.

CHAPTER NINE

THE MORNING AFTER

SOMETIMES SEX IS just sex. For Anna and Roger, that was the case: something to release stress at the end of a long day on a set or after working out.

But for Mark and Anna, they both knew something more guided the divine pleasure they experienced in being together. Anna had never felt so safe, and there was something about a man who had literally seen her down to her physical core that felt so unusual and amazing to her, she couldn't quite put it into words.

For Mark—besides being the first time he had been inside a woman in eons—he felt like he was home, not in the comfortable slippers sense of the word, but like his own heart had found its resting place. He couldn't get over Anna's natural beauty—a loveliness that was somewhat weathered by life and time and experiences—but those qualities only made her more exquisite to him.

His ex-wife hadn't loved him for a long while by the time they decided to part ways, and he realized he had missed knowing that a woman he entered wanted him so much it made her hurt. They had had each other three times that evening, with Mark being careful not to lay on top of her still-healing body, but the pure ecstasy of just being with one another that way made nothing else really matter.

Anna slept over Saturday night, and on Sunday, they went out for brunch at a quiet Santa Monica café where she was less likely to be jumped at by paparazzi. She hid her hair under a large hat and wore dark sunglasses, aware that Scofield wasn't used to their in-your-face ways or the tidal wave of publicity that could follow, especially once something made Page Six of the New York Post.

She knew she couldn't protect him from it forever, and after all, he was a grown man and made his own decisions, but she also didn't want to wake him from the adoring reverie he was in now. He sat with her small hand in his at the outdoor café, gently caressing her fingers because he couldn't believe this was all really happening. He wanted to memorize everything about her for when she wasn't by his side.

He smiled softly at her, saying nothing except with his eyes that never stopped looking at her. Anna loved it, but didn't want to show how much, so she looked away towards the beach, commenting on silly people walking by.

Anna knew that Roger would be coming home the next day, and wondered how that would play out, because the actress knew she would never have sex with the trainer again. It was time for the Brit to move out and move on. But she couldn't just kick him out with no warning and nowhere to go, so she had to think this through.

"This is going to be dicey for a while, you know," she said earnestly to the doctor, who didn't want to think about reality until Monday's patients were in his office.

"I need to end things with my boyfriend, of course. Really, it's been over for a while and we've both just been too lazy to cut the cord," Anna added, looking off towards the water. She turned back and looked straight into Mark's eyes when she said, "I won't be with him anymore, don't worry about that. It was never anything anyway."

Scofield would have been lying if he said it didn't matter to him. He absolutely wanted Anna to himself in the most caveman-like way. He wanted to possess her physically and emotionally, and to know she had his heart as carefully tucked away and protected as he did hers. But he couldn't say any of that after one weekend together, of course.

"I understand," he said, also looking off, so as not to betray the fact that he would have happily beaten Roger Niles into the ground at that moment and buried him in dirt, so he would never be seen again. "Do what you have to do."

After brunch, they went back to Scofield's house and made love two more times, both of them feeling like a perfect symphony of connectedness with each caress. After showering and changing back into her shirt dress, Anna let the doctor do what he had wanted to do for so long now: pick her up in his arms and carry her to his car.

"I better leave the tulips here," Anna said wistfully, sighing, as she stroked the lavish bouquets on his dining room table. "It might cause too many questions I'm not ready to answer."

Scofield said nothing as he carried her. Truthfully, if she had moved in with him at that moment, it would have made him the happiest man on Earth. The thought of not sleeping next to her that night and going back to just self-pleasuring was depressing to the doctor. He'd come home to an empty house for so long and gotten used to it, until now.

Once he slid Anna into the passenger seat and buckled her

up like a precious child, he came around and hopped into the driver's side of his Porsche. He could at least take a longer route to extend his time with her, so he drove the coast highway and pulled over at a scenic overlook.

He stopped the car and turned to look at her. "I just want you to know that I don't see this as a casual situation," he said softly. "I want to see you again and again and again. I hope you feel the same way," he added, swallowing as he said it and wondering if he sounded too insecure. Anna said nothing, but just nodded slightly and smiled.

She reached over and took his hand to her lips and kissed it, a move that seemed so sensual to Mark that he would have ravished her right there, but for her fragile and recovering body.

Instead, he leaned over, pulled her to him gently, and kissed her as passionately as he ever had a woman. "I love you," he blurted out and felt immediately sheepish for having shown his hand so early on. But Anna, still not speaking, just mouthed back with no sound "I love you, too" and they stared into each other's eyes for what seemed like a decade before Mark put the car back into gear and continued down the coast highway to Anna's Malibu home.

CHAPTER 10

RUDE AWAKENINGS

ROGER PULLED INTO the driveway late Monday afternoon, tired after his long weekend conference that had included twice as many workouts as he would normally have done with clients, and he was over it. He looked forward to some quick, easy sex with Anna, followed by a nap, and was already semi-erect when he walked into the house from the garage.

"Babe!" he yelled as he entered, but was met with no response. He walked into the airy bedroom and saw her back to him, curled up under a blanket. He thought how perfect this was, he could just sneak right in next to her and grab a quick afternooner before joining her in that long-awaited nap.

Anna awoke startled and turned to see Roger getting undressed. Hoping to distract him, she sat up and asked how his trip went.

"Fine, baby, fine," he said, jumping naked next to her into the bed, a move which made Anna viscerally pull away. "What's the matter?" Roger asked, pulling her shoulder, which hurt her still-fragile back. "You've always liked a little afternoon action before."

"Not now, please," Anna said, getting out of bed. But Niles refused to let it go.

"I've been gone four days and never touched a single 20-year-old," he said, as if this were a seductive statement. "Don't I deserve a little reward at least?"

"I said not now," Anna said firmly, turning to look at him coldly. "Actually, I've done a lot of thinking while you were away, and I want you to move out. It's not working anymore."

Roger stopped, grabbed a towel around his waist, and his expression changed. "Move out? To where? Who's going to train you?" he asked, his voice rising. There was a pause, and then he moved closer to her and dropped the towel. "Is it that doctor? Is that what this is about?" He grabbed her shoulder and as strong as he was, and as much pain as she was in, she couldn't get away from his grip and started to cry.

"Let me go, please," Anna begged, not wanting to look Roger in the face. He was pressing his body against her now and she could feel his well-endowed erection against her fragile frame that had just a short t-shirt and panties on.

"In a second, just let me get my rocks off," Roger said, picking her up and thrusting inside her. Anna screamed and started beating on his chiseled shoulders, but the trainer just laughed. "You like this, I know you do," he said, thrusting harder and harder, as Anna sobbed and screamed.

He was done quickly, and when he put her back on her feet, she could feel his semen pouring down her leg and wanted to vomit.

"Get out of my house now," she said icily. "I mean right now."

Anna grabbed a robe, ran into the massive master bath

and locked the door before turning on the shower as hot as she could stand it. She stood there sobbing hysterically for at least 30 minutes as the water drowned her out, and then just sat at the bathroom window that looked out on the beach and felt herself go numb. She slept curled up on pillows in her enormous adjoining master closet that night, still locked in.

She'd left her phone on the bedside table, and didn't get any of Mark's five text messages asking if she was okay.

∽

At daybreak, Anna stealthily opened the door to the master bedroom from the bathroom, and saw a note lying on her pillow. She wasn't ready to read it, so she picked up her phone, saw the multiple messages from Mark and her heart sank. How would she explain this to him and would it end their barely breathing love affair?

She looked out the window, saw that Roger's car was gone, and immediately called a locksmith. Then she trepadaciously opened the note, cringing as she read it.

Anna:

I've never done anything but take care of you, so not sure where all of this came from. It seems so sudden. I couldn't get most of my clothes out since you locked yourself in the bathroom. I already have a place to stay with a friend, will swing by and get the rest of my stuff soon. No hard feelings, I hope.

Roger

She couldn't believe it, reading the note that was written as if nothing wrong had happened the night before at all. Was he pretending or did he really think he hadn't sexually assaulted her? she wondered.

But far worse right now, Anna knew this scenario could read horribly wrong if she told Mark and he misunderstood what had happened.

He might think she'd wanted to sleep with Roger, but then make it look like she hadn't so she could have her cake and eat it, too. Of course, he'd have no way of knowing anything had happened, except for the lack of text responses on her part. But she knew she had to tell him something.

Knowing it wasn't a surgery day and that Mark wouldn't be in his office until 9 a.m., Anna texted Mark carefully, thinking about every word she typed, and hoping not to alarm him.

"Something bad happened yesterday after he got home," she wrote, unable to call Roger either by his name or refer to him as her boyfriend ever again. "He's gone now and I'm waiting for the locksmith. Please don't think badly of me. I love you."

She pressed "send" and held her breath. It was only 6 a.m. and Mark was at the gym working out before he went into the office, but a minute didn't pass before he called her.

"What did that bastard do to you?" he said, his voice sounding like a tornado gathering force. "I'm coming over." He felt helpless and enraged all at once.

Anna knew men well enough to know this could go from bad to worse if the two men crossed paths. And knowing that Roger knew martial arts and that Scofield—who wrote prescriptions for the most coveted of all legal drugs, opioids—carried a legally permitted concealed weapon, just made it that much more dangerous.

"No, no, I'm ok, really," Anna said, fighting back tears that Mark could hear in her voice. "You need to go see your patients, don't worry about me. I have a locksmith coming over any minute, so he won't be able to get back in."

Suddenly Anna started sobbing and dropped the phone on the bed. At that exact moment, the doorbell rang: the locksmith had arrived.

She opened the door in a robe, looking like a mess. But her tear-stained face didn't move the young man: he'd seen it a million times. In Los Angeles, even among the very wealthy and celebrities, domestic abuse was as common as fake boobs, and he'd become inured to it completely.

"You needed some locks changed, ma'am?" he said. He was 25 if a day and didn't recognize Anna in her current state, if he would have anyway.

"Yes, please, all of them, and do it quickly, please." she added.

She wiped her face with the back of her robe. "Forgive my appearance, it's been a bad stretch," Anna said, suddenly wincing at how badly her back was hurting.

CHAPTER 11

RACING HEARTS

MARK KNEW HE had enough time to drive quickly to Anna's home and still make the office—if maybe 20 minutes late—even allowing for him to shower and change at her house first. He jumped in his car, still in his sweaty t-shirt and shorts, and pushed the Porsche to do what it was designed to do, barely beating the coast highway rush hour traffic.

His car screeched into the driveway and he jumped out like a fireman on a three-alarmer. Scofield ran to the door, which was open, with the locksmith already doing his work, and called "Anna?!"

She wanted to run, but instead collapsed on the floor. "Anna?!" the doctor yelled again and then pushed past the boy and ran into the house. She was lying in the hallway, passed out.

"I need to take this woman to the hospital," Scofield barked brusquely at the locksmith. He pulled $500 in cash out of his wallet and handed it to the kid. "Make sure all these locks get changed. If this doesn't cover it," he said, grabbing a business card and shoving it at the young man, "call my office and we'll make sure you get the balance. Oh, and drop off all the keys in an envelope with my name on it."

"Yes, sir," the locksmith said, pocketing the Benjamins. Normally, it would have been reckless to leave a stranger with access to a movie star's Malibu pad, but there was nothing normal about what had just happened and the doctor had no choice.

Mark swept Anna up as if she were a feather, placed her in the passenger seat of his car and sped off to UCLA in Santa Monica. It would be at least a 45-minute drive, but there was no way to go but to take the coast highway to get there. Her head was slumped over, and he tried taking her pulse while he drove. It was slow, but not alarming, and he suspected that shock had kicked in over whatever had transpired the night before.

Scofield called his office and told them about the locksmith without saying it wasn't for his own home. He indicated he had a medical emergency and would likely be not only late, but possibly out of the office all morning. He then called his front desk manager at her home and asked her to try to reschedule all of his morning appointments.

Finally, he called Paul to meet him at UCLA as quickly as possible.

✑

If Scofield had been concerned that Crawford might notice something was different about him that Monday morning, he certainly hadn't anticipated meeting his wing man with the woman of his dreams actually laying in his arms in a bathrobe, passed out.

He pulled into the emergency entrance, and being a known doctor at the hospital with surgical privileges, was able to sweep past all the usual sign-in mayhem and get Anna onto a gurney and taken upstairs for MRIs, X-rays, and some medication, as well as a complete blood workup.

He thought if they found anything bad, he would hunt down that monster and push him off a Malibu cliff.

"What happened?" Paul asked when he pulled open the curtain surround of the ER exam room.

"I'm not sure, exactly," Scofield said. "She called me this morning very early and told me something bad had happened with her live-in boyfriend, but that she was ok. I went to her house to check on her, and she had collapsed," said the doctor, realizing even as he told this accurate tale that it sounded full of holes and questions, and could possibly even put his own actions of the day before into question.

After all, they'd made love twice on Sunday, and she could easily still have Mark's semen inside her if they did a rape kit, which they most certainly would, based on his initial information to law enforcement. It could end up being a very thorny situation for him, with no one but Anna herself to vouch for the doctor. And in California, a man could be arrested and charged without his partner pressing charges: it happened all the time.

A female cop came in and took more background from him as the ER staff administered the rape kit to collect semen. Anna was now hooked up to a glucose IV and starting to come to. He could see the pain on her face, and guessed that her muscles had taken a bad downturn from the entire traumatic experience.

"Hook her up to some morphine, stat," Scofield said, suddenly finding some degree of calm in his doctor persona.

He told Paul to order an MRI and X-ray to make sure her fusion and spinal screws were all intact. He could see the confusion in Paul's eyes, as well as his assistant's mind trying to piece the whole scenario together, and he knew he'd have a lot of explaining to do once the immediate crisis had passed.

CHAPTER 12

TESTING, TESTING

THE FILMS CAME back showing no new serious trauma to her back, which relieved Scofield enormously. He'd checked Anna in at his own expense for now, to make sure she was monitored for at least 24 hours and also to be certain that Roger would have no access to her. He instructed all the hospital personnel on the ortho ward not to let anyone but himself or Paul and hospital nursing staff into her room, and to let the doctor know if anyone else tried.

He didn't even know Roger's name, let alone what he did or where he might be. If he needed to hire some security to guard her and her house for a while, so be it. Mark wasn't about to lose the only woman who'd stirred his heart in nearly two decades to some abuser, that was for sure.

He wished he had a picture of the guy to show hospital staff and security, but didn't want to upset Anna, who was now conscious, if woozy, from the morphine drip. It was already 10 a.m. and by now he'd told his office the whole day might have to be rescheduled due to a medical emergency he had to attend to. These things did happen, so he knew no one but Paul would question the situation later.

Mark sat down by Anna's bed, which was raised so that she was in a three-quarters sitting position. Her eyes were dazed from the intravenous drip, but he could at least see she was not in pain anymore, and for the moment, it would numb the emotional trauma as well. He had given the female cop his contact info and told her what he knew. But he was afraid to upset Anna now by asking her anymore.

"Hey sweetheart," he said softly, sitting by her bed and holding her hand gently. She was on an IV glucose drip as well, and also catheterized so she could just rest. "How are you feeling? You scared me there, baby girl."

Anna turned her head and smiled towards him with her eyes only half-opened. "I feel ok now," she slurred. "What happened?" He suddenly realized the shock had caused some kind of temporary amnesia, which was going to make the whole situation much stickier, but he couldn't worry about that at present.

"We're not totally sure, honey. You called me very upset about your boyfriend who had come home, and I rushed over and found you collapsed in the hallway, you'd passed out. I rushed you to the ER. You're going to be fine. We checked all your vitals and did scans, and everything is ok that way.

"You just need to rest now. The hospital staff will take good care of you when I can't be here. They're probably going to release you tomorrow, I'll have surgery, but I'll hire a nurse to stay with you and make sure you're ok. I had the locksmith leave the new keys to your house with my office, and I'm going to keep one too."

Anna had no filter and no game in her current state, and just squeezed his hand and kept smiling. "My knight in shining armor," she said, sounding drunk. Then she closed her eyes and drifted off.

Scofield knew he had to go back to her house with the new keys, make sure it was secured and protected, and get all of Roger's belongings out before Anna could ever go back.

CHAPTER 13

DARK SHADOWS

U NBEKNOWNST TO ANNA, Nile's unwelcome advances that weekend were not the first time he had gone too far with a woman and ignored her pleas to stop.

When he was 16, Roger had been arrested in London—where he grew up—for raping a 15-year-old girl. As with Anna, it had been a girlfriend, but she told her parents and police were called. Ultimately, the charges were dropped due to lack of concrete proof to bring the case forward, but Roger was told in no uncertain terms to stay away from her forever.

Because of the dropped charges and his age at the time, nothing ever showed up on a criminal record for the trainer, which would have kept him from being able to go stateside whatsoever.

∞

The morning after the sexual assault, Roger considered what Anna might do in the light of day, and decided not to wait for a call from the Malibu division of the L.A. Sheriff's department, asking him to come in for questioning. He had no idea if he'd left any marks or bruises on the actress's delicate frame, but realized it was entirely possible.

With the relationship over anyway, he didn't want to risk a trial, and maybe even jail time.

But Scofield knew none of this, and Niles wasn't about to leave a note for anyone. So, when Mark entered Anna's home with the new keys the locksmith had brought to his office, he went through every door and her entire master closet looking for anything he could put in a huge trash bag. He figured eventually he could deliver it all to some friend of the trainer, and that he could determine who that would be later on.

Men do not like the scent of another man on what they consider theirs. Every shirt, pair of shoes or pants, hat or socks that the doctor found of Roger's, he wanted to destroy.

Mark shoved Roger's belongings into three enormous lawn trash bags and threw them into the back seat of his sports car. If there is one thing a Porsche is not designed for, it's moving merchandise, but he had to take it. He could put it in his garage until Anna could get him a contact number and an address later.

◦◦◦

Anna was sitting up in her hospital bed by the next day and eating, though not very much. The morphine drip was gone and she was back on muscle relaxers and Tylenol, the standard treatment after spinal fusion surgery.

She felt sore all over, and couldn't remember much of what had actually happened. Bits and pieces would float into her mind and she would push them back down again. The actress felt safe from Roger as long as she was in the hospital, and knew Mark would come check on her that evening at her home.

He'd had his own front desk receptionist drop off her new key to Anna at the hospital, and kept three copies for himself to ensure that the extras didn't get lost when she checked out, or stolen by hospital staff.

You couldn't be too careful anymore, especially when a well-known celebrity was involved.

By 1 p.m., Anna was given the official okay from a hospital doctor that Scofield knew to go home. Mark had insisted on a trusted male nurse he knew to accompany her and stay there until he got there, both for her own safety and so that Anna wouldn't be afraid and alone. The nurse drove her home in his own small car and helped her walk shakily into the beach house.

Everything looked in order, and Mark had already texted her that he believed he'd gotten everything out that belonged to Roger. She was both relieved and nervous not to have had a word from the Brit since the note on her bed the morning after the attack. Mark had taken it for safekeeping and so as not to have her upset when she returned to the house.

No reason to stir bad memories now, he thought. There would be plenty of time for recall with detectives once she was more stabilized.

Anna lay down and found herself fighting sleep, even though she was exhausted. She was afraid Roger might break a window if he came back and realized his keys were no good anymore. She made hot tea and sat in the living room with the nurse watching the Food Network to distract herself. Mark texted her at around 4 o'clock that his surgeries were running late, but that he would be at her house before 9 p.m.

She felt relief and gratitude that he cared so much. It wasn't a position Anna had ever been in throughout her life. She was used to having to watch her own back, and now she had someone to do it for her, both literally and figuratively. It was something she had dreamed about often as a young girl, but such a hero seemed so unlikely back then, she wasn't surprised when none had ever materialized.

Until now.

CHAPTER 14

BAD MEMORIES

ANNA HAD GROWN up in central California, the eldest of two in a family of very modest means. They lived in Merced, where her father worked on a huge commercial poultry farm. It was a gruesome factory and her father smelled like death every single day when he returned home from work. But the uneducated man was lucky to have any employment at all in the turbulent 1960s, and over time, the daily slaughter and cruelty to animals became normalized in his own mind.

Mrs. Porter—Anna's mother—drank bottom-shelf vodka daily, and started her drinking early in the morning. Although it was only Anna and her much-younger brother Jerrod, the woman felt overwhelmed, and hated her husband, who came home smelling like blood and animal shit and wanted to have sex with her after his shift almost daily, without even showering first.

One night, Anna's mother refused his advances and threw a dirty plate at his head, drawing blood. Enraged, her father grabbed his wife's vodka bottle and poured half of it down his own throat all at once, causing a near-blackout. In that state, he went into Anna's room and raped his then 10-year-old daughter for the first time.

She had already learned to be silent when her mother went into an alcoholic tirade, and applied the same strategy to her father, just hoping it would be over soon. Anna had no idea what the sticky stuff was that ran down her leg afterwards, but knew it was something shameful. She wiped it away with a t-shirt which she threw in the trash outside, wrapping it inside tissues. It smelled as bad as her father's overalls.

Anna threw up that night—and for many subsequent nights thereafter—when her father repeated his sexual assaults against her over and over and over, causing her to be wraith-thin as she moved towards adolescence.

It became hard for to keep food down at all, in fact, and sharing a meal with her parents and brother was so torturous for the young girl that she would usually find any reason to escape it. Neither her mother nor father ever tried to convince her to sit down, as each had their own dark secrets that were easier to avoid without having to look at the pained child they had spawned and abused and neglected.

Anna's mother, meanwhile—having found some freedom from the man she detested, at least in her own bed—continued to refuse his advances, and Porter's visits to his daughter's bedroom became commonplace. The child did not dare tell her mother, knowing that she wouldn't believe her anyway and would probably beat her and tell Anna she was a liar.

The visits continued, even when Anna began menstruating at 13. Already a very slender beauty who got attention wherever she went, she watched the small, flickering black-and-white family TV and dreamed of being a dancer or an actress like the ones she saw on the Ed Sullivan and Jackie Gleason shows.

But it was a world so removed from her own that it might as well have been Mars or Pluto, and Anna could not have known then that sooner rather than later, she would indeed be on her way to Hollywood.

⁓

One day, Mrs. Porter told her daughter that she was going to visit her own sister in Iowa and wasn't sure when she would be back. She told Anna to watch her then three-year-old brother and to cook for her father when he came home.

Sensing her only chance to escape—and not wanting to be raped yet again by her father—Anna left her sleeping brother Jerrod and her home as soon as her mother was out of sight, and hitchhiked to the coast and Hollywood, getting raped four times in the process.

She assumed it was the price she had to pay for freedom. And after all, it was nothing new to her anyway, and at least these men didn't smell of dried blood and chicken shit.

CHAPTER 15

FACING LIFE ALONE

T HE CASTING COUCH is likely as old a concept as show business itself, and one thing Anna ironically had on her side was already being groomed to handle both the reality of rape and what men wanted to assuage their sexual desires. So even at 13, the young beauty was helped by producers who did whatever they wanted to her and had her blow their dicks in exchange for small roles in B movies.

Anna was often given some money for her submission, another perk of tolerating the advances of men who were invariably at least three times her age. She knew nothing else and just assumed it was a normal way of life. She would usually find a cheap motel—or sometimes just sleep in a back alley —depending on how generous the predators had been and how many had assaulted her in a week.

༄

By the time she was 17, the young actress had a bevy of producer johns who paid some of her bills and gave her increasingly larger parts as she became more suitable to play them. Her reading skills were sketchy, since she hadn't had much of an education, but Anna improved over time with help from other actors and even a tutor that one producer arranged to help her memorize lines.

Her refined beauty belied her rough childhood, and she was cast as princesses, ballerinas and socialites, all roles in which she felt finally at home, exactly because they were all so fantastical to her.

Anna's imagination saved her, and she lived in it whenever she could, blocking out the memory of her parents and brother and her life in Merced. No one ever tried to find her—at least that she knew of—and the girl quickly crafted a story about being orphaned at a young age and left to fend for herself. The story played into many a producer's rape fantasies about helpless young girls and fed their egos into believing they were actually helping her, instead of abusing her.

The budding actress had already mastered turning off her emotions while pretending to turn them on when it served her, and no one outside of the girl's own head could have told the difference between what she really felt and what was an act: a convenient skill set for a young thespian, indeed.

As a result, Anna Porter continued to rise in the industry, and by 18, was starting to build a name for herself, helped by whoever her latest producer-rapist happened to be.

CHAPTER 16

BLOWING IT

I N THE LATE 1970s—when Anna came of age in Hollywood—cocaine was everywhere. At every party, in every producer's office, even at some table reads, the powdery white substance that was all the rage made its presence felt.

But for the young actress who had seen what addiction did to both of her parents—and who knew that her stunning good looks and keeping her wits about her were her primary ticket out of the hell of her childhood—coke held no allure. Neither did alcohol or pot, for that matter. She steadfastly refused to partake in any of them, telling those who offered her any of these substances that she had extreme allergies, so as not to sound like she was judging them.

The only kind of blow that Anna regularly partook in were the near-ubiquitous requests from any man in town who had the power to grant or kill a gig for her and who were thrilled to see her get down on her knees as they unzipped their pants. Anna was numb to them by this time, and would simply make the sounds and movements she knew were required to pass the hurdles and get the job they had promised her for sucking their dicks.

The actress had no close friends. She trusted no one and would never have revealed her true past to anybody. Once she turned 18, Anna breathed easier, knowing nobody could ever make her go home again. She had no idea if her father, mother or brother were even still alive, let alone if her parents had ever sought her whereabouts.

⁂

There were hundreds of blow jobs and just as many bit parts behind her when Anna finally landed her first starring role in a movie at 22 years old.

Her looks were reminiscent of a slimmer, softer and more delicate Ava Gardner, and she sizzled on screen. The camera—which captures not just great beauty, but also something haunted in the eyes of many a Hollywood star—loved her, and so did audiences. Men wanted to fuck her and women wanted her good looks and incredibly slender frame, and her stardom rose quickly from that first big role.

When she was cast as the romantic lead in a movie opposite Grant Houston—a 30-year-old star who had seen her on some sets and suggested to the director that she be cast as his love interest—she knew she had truly arrived. Along with the part, of course, came the predictable servicing of Houston in his trailer, but Anna considered that a small price to pay to move up in the world and start making real money of her own at last.

CHAPTER 17

BREAKING DOWN THE WALL

D R. MARK SCOFIELD'S childhood had been nothing like Anna's. Born into an upper-middle class Midwestern family, his father was a college professor and his mother a stay-at-home mom. Along with his four brothers—of whom Mark was the eldest—the future doctor enjoyed playing all the usual sports like football and baseball growing up, and with his good looks and good manners, had the trifecta of qualities to attract any pretty girl he wanted in high school.

Ironically, he was incredibly picky about who he took out even then, which, of course, only added to his allure for the girls in his class, and even in grades above and below his own.

As a student, Mark showed an early aptitude for biology and math, and scored 142 on his IQ test in his junior year of high school, putting him at the "near genius or genius" level, far above his peers and in just a fraction of one percent of all humans around the globe.

His teachers told his parents that he belonged in the best school in the country, and with his incredibly high scores and

IQ, he was accepted into Harvard as an undergraduate. He immediately started studying for what he would need to move on to the university's prestigious medical school, and with a work ethic that had been instilled in him from a young age by his stern and strict father, Scofield graduated college in just two-and-a-half years at the top of his class, and moved on to his medical studies at barely 20 years old.

Mark had always excelled at everything he touched: sports, science, medicine, and yes, women. His need to feel connected eliminated many girls who would have easily made the cut for most men in his enviable position, but the young doctor-to-be had no interest in someone who didn't make his pulse go up as high as his dick.

He spent so much time studying once he hit medical school that dating was low on his list of priorities. When his fellow medical students would talk about the women they'd bedded, he would walk away, finding it unclassy and distasteful.

His father had told him to control his sexual impulses from the time he could remember, warning Mark about what would happen if the young man got a girl pregnant or picked up a venereal disease. Combined with his family position as the golden child who would excel in medicine, Mark felt no attraction for most of the girls who would have happily thrown themselves at him had he given them the slightest encouragement.

But he was not without both curiosity and hormones, and turned largely to masturbation to relieve the intense sexual cravings that overtook him several times a day. He learned to be covert about his self-pleasuring, and soon realized that it gave him a power to resist otherwise attractive women who might have taken him off course, or derail his dreams of going to medical school and having a successful practice one day.

Eventually, that power to be able to resist many of the

beautiful and tempting women who came his way as a neuro-surgeon became useful. Other men—who were less restrained in their natural urges—often paid the price with increasingly expensive divorces and public scandals as the years went by.

Every wall can be knocked down with enough force, however. Anna's arrival in Mark's life was not the first brick to be thrown at his, but it was the largest, and by far the most powerful.

⌗

When Anna first came into Scofield's office complaining of severe pain up and down her right leg, he recognized her immediately. Having four years on him, she had been just older enough when she got her early starring roles to have mesmerized the dedicated college student. It was something about how fragile she looked that had gripped him, physically—but more than that—emotionally.

The future doctor—being the eldest of five and with his medical acumen—was a natural fixer. Anything with a broken wing or fractured leg that he found down by the stream near his house growing up, he would bring home to treat and heal. It gave him pleasure to figure out how to take something shattered and make it to grow back together, and then watch it fly—or run—back to its natural habitat.

His parents were used to him carrying in birds, squirrels, and one time, even a baby deer. When Mark first laid eyes on her, Anna reminded him of that deer: doe-eyed and teetering on her slender legs from pain. Mostly, he thought—as he looked at her effortless loveliness—she needed to be taken care of. And that's what Mark did best. He needed to protect and heal someone, and get them better than he'd found them, and in Anna, he sensed another broken creature who desperately required his care.

There was immediate electricity between them, and the doctor tried not to get distracted as he felt her leg up and down, asking where the pain was worst, while looking at her MRI to match what she said was hurting against what he saw. Scofield knew almost immediately that she would need surgery, and couldn't help but be happy, because that meant he would have numerous more times to see her, speak to her, and touch her.

He had her lift the back of her chiffony blouse so he could run his hands down her spine, resting almost at her butt. She seemed not at all uncomfortable, and it took all of his self-control to take his hands off of her soft white skin when he was done examining her. The bones on her back jutted out a bit, because she was so slender, which he also found oddly alluring.

Scofield was generous with his time with his patients, even if it meant the waiting room was always full. But that first day, he spent even longer than usual with Anna, drinking in her exquisiteness.

"You're going to need to get this taken care of, and I wouldn't wait too long either," he told her earnestly. Anna knew she had a film coming up, of course. Even after so many years in the business, she still didn't take making good money for granted, and the thought of losing—or even just postponing—a gig made her nervous.

She lived in a $12 million-dollar beachfront Malibu home that was paid for. Anna had chosen the beach because the water smelled so different from her father, and the sound of lapping waves because they drowned out her memories of his horrible breath and the disgusting things he said as he raped her.

Scofield, of course, knew none of this when he met Anna. He only sensed that he was needed, and in more ways than one.

༄

Almost exactly as promised, Mark showed up at Anna's Malibu home that night, just after nine o'clock. She'd been sleeping for hours, and was slightly startled when he quietly tiptoed into the dark house, using his key, as she was afraid it might be Roger.

The nurse was still there, watching TV, and left once the doctor arrived.

Mark turned on one entry light so she could see who it was and then quickly came over to the sofa where she lay on pillows in a cotton negligee that he could almost see her breasts through. He wanted so much to make love to her, but knew she was both physically and emotionally fragile, so held back.

He kissed her forehead and sat down on the floor next to where she was lying, still horizontal with her hands tucked under her head and her hair pulled back in a soft and loose ponytail.

"Hey sweetheart, how are you feeling?" Mark asked, gently stroking her hair and wishing he could stroke something else as well. "Have you eaten anything today?"

She realized she had had nothing since she left the hospital earlier. Anna had probably lost five pounds since the surgery and was almost painfully thin, her hip bones jutting out too far under her taut ivory skin.

She shook her head in the negative and he asked her what she would be able to eat. Anna always lost her appetite when under duress. She blew through her lips as people do when frustrated and shrugged.

"Can you just hold me?" she whispered to Mark, sitting up slowly and looking into his eyes. He wanted to melt and wrapped his arms around her, grasping her tiny body tightly but gingerly between his strong hands. She started to sob on his shoulder and he felt both amazing and powerless, all at once, for her trusting him enough to show her feelings and because he could do nothing to quell them.

"It's ok, honey," he said, caressing the back of her hair and whispering into her ear softly. "I'm here. Nobody's going to hurt you ever again."

He felt his own tears welling up, but brushed them away before she could see them or feel them on her cheek. She clung to him like a raft in a stormy sea, as if for dear life. When she finally pulled away, her face looked swollen from crying. He wiped away the tears and kissed her forehead and then her lips, as gently as he could.

She didn't pull back though, to his surprise, but instead kissed him back more passionately. Anna had never known feelings like she had for Mark, and it was a secret treasure box that had been opened. His lack of wanting anything from her but her heart and soul, or pressuring her in any way sexually, allowed her—for the very first time in her life—to actually want a man, physically and emotionally, completely, totally, and of her own free will.

Scofield couldn't resist her passion, and gave in to his own. She cried out when she came and he held her and kissed her over and over and over again.

⁓

Roger Niles had landed at Heathrow with very few physical possessions. He had grabbed $10,000 out of a drawer in Anna's house and whatever of his that was lying in the bedroom, along with a few pieces of Anna's jewelry that she had casually left on her nightstand by the bed. He planned to pawn them later.

He had no real plan, but his mother was still living outside of London. He hoped to stay with her while he figured out his next move.

Roger had grown up in a rough hood in London's down-trodden East End. His father had been a train conductor in the Underground subway system, and his mother took in the children of working parents to help pay for expenses, forcing Roger to often both defend himself against their bullying and just fend for himself generally.

He got into numerous fights with the live-in daycare kids and quickly toughened up. The scruffy kid often skipped school and instead, took to building up his strength by boxing other boys in the streets. There was no money for any kind of formal training for the then-scrawny Roger.

Because of his street fighting, by 14, Niles' physique had more than made up for his lean childhood, and he was more muscular and buff than most teenage boys. By the time he turned 21, he easily drew the attention of bored upper middle-class wives and divorcees who were willing to subsidize his lifestyle in exchange for sex and being their arm candy at events that their husbands (or lack thereof) were absent from.

By 23, Roger was a familiar sight at the higher-end gyms these ladies worked out in religiously, and started training both his girlfriends and their friends, slowly building a chichi clientele.

His chiseled good looks and constant dark stubble appealed to women more used to the pasty and pale refinement of British upper-crust gentlemen, and his perfect eight-pack abs—which he always displayed shirtless while training—didn't hurt his drawing power, either.

Roger had raised himself, emotionally speaking, and lacked the refinement or knowledge of the manners of the British upper classes.

He also lacked any finesse in bed, having no sensuality whatsoever, and spent as little time on foreplay as possible, preferring to cut to the chase and just stick his dick into whatever honeypot happened to be with him at the moment. Many women felt his complete insensitivity to their needs was justified, believing it stemmed from them not being pretty or thin enough: a belief he did nothing to dispel.

The truth was, Niles had no emotional language for any of that, and it bored him to even hear about it. He smoked covertly—a habit picked up in his youth to appear tough—but generally hid it from his ladies and saved it for a local pub in his old hood where there was zero chance of him running into anyone he might be bedding at the moment.

⌒

Roger had first met Anna six years earlier, when she was in London for a movie premiere. He was with a beautiful but boring socialite and watched the actress from across the red carpet. He saw women largely as belt notches, and decided he had to have the petite American actress to add one more. He had become proud of his lineup of trophy women, which by the time he hit 40, easily topped 350.

He flashed his perfectly veneered white teeth at her just as the paparazzi flashed incessantly in her face, and ticked his head back in one of those "come meet me later" universal gestures that men use with women when they are being slick.

At the party after the premiere—where Roger's date got drunk and sloppy and Anna's agent worked the room making business connections—the trainer made his move. He'd learned over the years, simply by trial and error, that a softer approach worked better with women of a certain class.

He was unaware that Anna came from as rough a background as he did, of course, and could only go by her refined appearance and how she carried herself. Thus, he assumed she was of the American upper classes, born and bred.

He knew a cheesy line about her beauty would be a yawner.

Anna Porter, the movie star, had undoubtedly heard them all thousands of times. So he decided to go for some humor instead to break the ice.

"The movie was amazing," he said, swizzling a gin and tonic and not even looking right at her, although he stood as close to her as he could. "These premieres are all the same though. Just beautiful women and horny men, every damned time," he said, turning at that moment to grin at her, which actually made her laugh at its accuracy.

Anna surveyed the room filled with potbellied middle-aged men in tuxes and exceedingly long-legged and slender 20-something beauties in loaned-out haute couture gowns and millions of dollars in borrowed diamonds fawning at them for attention.

"Do you know what the definition of a gentleman is?" Roger said, turning to really look at her. "A wolf who can wait," he answered his own joke, before she could say anything. With that, he winked at her and walked off. He knew that such a move was bound to arouse interest in a woman used to constantly arousing interest—and fending off aggressive attempts at sexual connections—from men.

⁓

The Brit and the American didn't see each other again for six months, until one of Roger's lady friends—a recently divorced ex-pat American—paid for him to come with her to Santa Barbara for the summer. She covered all of his expenses, from his travel to his upscale wardrobe to his required grooming. Several times, they drove down to L.A., and on one such trip, drove into Malibu to visit with one of the socialite's old friends.

Stopping at an overpriced market to load up on healthy food, Roger and his lady friend went searching for items in different aisles, where lo and behold, he looked over the organic produce display to see the lovely Anna Porter squeezing a large organic tomato.

He grinned cheekily and started laughing in his deep baritone. "It appears the wolf waited too long, eh?" he said, making Anna smile at the simple fact that he remembered the last corny words he had thrown at her. "But wolves show up at the front door when least expected," he added, looking up at her almost ominously. "Might this one knock on yours someday?" he added.

Anna had no need to affirm her good looks with additional male attention, even if she was getting older, and just smiled and shrugged. At that moment, Nile's blonde, 30-something girlfriend rounded the corner into their aisle, and he nonchalantly walked away from the produce, no longer acknowledging Anna whatsoever.

*

But the chase was on, and that was all it really was for Roger. It was a fox hunt to see how many beautiful women he could bag. Of course, he had no idea which Malibu home was Anna's, but he knew they were staying through the weekend in the area, and as luck would have it, for some political fundraisers over the next few days. He thought he might get lucky and catch her at one them. He had no idea if she had a significant other, but he planned to look irresistible at the events just in case she was single—or bedable, even if she was not.

Niles had been fitted out for several designer tuxes while in London. Thus, he showed up at the first event—also conveniently held in the Malibu Canyon at an $18-million-dollar luxury ocean-front home—dressed to the nines and looking far more debonair than he actually was.

Anna was also an attendee and showed up unaccompanied.

Roger struck up a conversation with the actress—being careful not to be so attentive that it would get his girlfriend's hackles up—and casually asked her if she lived nearby.

While movie stars may be wary of the general public's interest in their personal lives, once one has entered a certain invisible vector in the Hollywood inner sanctum, all walls come down and everyone becomes everyone else's bff. Anna had no reason not to trust this handsome Brit in the Tom Ford perfectly fitted tuxedo, and thus told him her address and gave him her cell number without any hesitation whatsoever.

She even mentioned that he and his girlfriend should come by for tea sometime when they were next in the area.

Roger mentioned that they would be in and out of L.A. for another few weeks—casually dropping the name of the owner of the lavish multimillion-dollar home in which the next fundraising soirée they would be attending was to be held—and with that, Anna's guard was completely down.

Those who have been sexually abused as children have only two emotional modes: completely guarded and utterly guileless. They have never learned the subtler distinctions of the cagey predator, the ones who don't pounce, so much as sneak up from behind and then trap and kill their prey in their unrelenting jaws, like crocodiles.

Because of that, Anna never saw Roger coming for her. He realized there was no reason to continue to amass British socialites when there were women like Anna across the pond. He also quickly understood there was far more potential business—and many more stunningly beautiful women to bed—in Southern California, than he was ever likely to find at home in London.

But Niles knew he could only stay stateside for 90 days unless he married his American ex-pat, who planned to return stateside permanently now. Being determined to make this move, he plotted out his strategy diligently.

⌒

Roger couldn't be too openly flirtatious with Anna while he was wooing his potential American bride, who was spending part of the summer searching out her own future Malibu beach house. Having come into her marriage with a trust fund, the typical cost of a home facing the ocean was not a problem for the leggy and slender Carey Morgenstern, Roger's travelling companion and the object of his marital focus.

Con men are thus named because of their ability to inspire confidence in their targeted victims, and at that, Niles was a master. Another trait of the professional in this regard is his innate instinct to sniff out those most likely to fall for their game. Carey—a beautiful but insecure 36-year-old sole beneficiary of a hedge-fund fortune from her now-deceased father—was the perfect target for the conniving trainer.

She'd been officially divorced for over a year now, having been cheated on and lied to by her also-dashing ex-husband—a British airline pilot—for years leading up to their split, and her thirst for approbation, both sexual and emotional, was virtually bottomless. Roger had learned the right things to say to women, in the same way that Anna had learned what to say to producers, and both had mastered the art of giving people what they wanted to hear, with no actual sincerity to back it up. But people thirsty to hear things a certain way are seldom capable of noticing the difference between honest and deceitful verbiage.

Niles spent the rest of the summer flooding his intended with every sentiment she'd ever craved from her mostly absent father and philandering ex-husband, and it worked like a charm. Walking on Rodeo Drive one day in late summer in

Beverly Hills, hand-in-hand, Roger got down on one knee and sprung the question to Morgenstern. He couldn't afford the kind of ring a woman of Carey's social status would expect—as they both well knew—but he was also aware that she would be happy to pick out and pay for her own on her black Amex card, as long as she felt he adored her.

⌒

Carey Morgenstern accepted Roger's proposal willingly, and they went ring shopping that very day at Harry Winston. They left with a $92,000 four-carat emerald-cut solitaire set in platinum, with simple matching bands for each of them for another $8,000.

The couple set a date for a small and quick ceremony before summer's end, to which Anna—who by now had met Carey at several social events—was ironically invited. It was held at an exclusive Malibu vineyard and included only 75 of Morgenstern's social circle, along with their spouses or significant others.

Anna brought her contract attorney as her date, an unexciting but trustworthy man whom she knew would not pressure her in any way to dance too close or cop a feel of her ass, or expect to get any action after the event was over, either.

⌒

Like many people born into extreme wealth and uninitiated in how those with less secure incomes may view such a status, Carey—against the advice of her own attorney—refused to make Roger sign a pre-nuptial agreement. They expedited his permanent resident status so that he could get a green card and get back to personal training, which Roger wanted as much to get him away from his endlessly insecure bride as anything else.

The freedom to work again—as well as the Lamborghini that Morgenstern gifted him as a wedding present—also got the Brit into the arms of an ever-expanding bevy of anxious Hollywood beauties determined to be thinner and fitter than the thousands of other young hopefuls who flooded into town year after year.

He remained on good behavior with his new bride—at least as far as she could determine—until his green card was granted and his permanent resident status solidified, plus a little bit longer to avoid any suspicion from US immigration authorities.

But by three years after his rapid wedding to Morgenstern, Roger's ennui at having to continually bolster her increasingly floundering ego as she pushed 40 caught up with him and he was discovered *in flagrante* by his wife one weekday afternoon in the couple's own master bedroom with a 20-something blonde client.

Humiliated and crushed, Carey filed for divorce the next day, but with California being a community property state and no pre-nup, she had to give Roger three million just to get rid of him quickly and with minimal tabloid coverage. She only got away with that relatively low amount because of their short time together, having no kids, and Roger being more than able-bodied enough to work. And, of course, also due to the heiress having far better legal representation than the dependent Brit could ever afford, making the outcome obvious.

While three million dollars might seem like a hefty nest egg, in L.A culture, it is barely upper-middle class. Roger, by this time, had developed a dependence on anabolic steroids, a popular testosterone-boosting substance that he obtained illegally to maintain his shredded physique as he approached 40.

The trainer had also been introduced to cocaine at several of the high-end social events he'd attended, a substance that would normally have been outside of his bankroll, but that he could now afford with his post-marital settlement. He loved the quick rush it gave him and how it enhanced his sex life with the many women he quickly fucked—and just as quickly tossed aside.

But the cost of the two illegal substances continually escalated for Niles, and combined with the realities of maintaining the high-end L.A. lifestyle of a notable personal trainer to the stars—including a gym to train them in—caught up with him more rapidly than he'd expected.

CHAPTER 18

HOOK, LINE AND SINK HER

PEOPLE RAISED IN poverty who get a taste of money later in life will almost invariably do anything to avoid returning to their former squalor, as was the case for both Anna and Roger. But Anna had been careful with her money over the years, and with no addictions to burn through her savings and a few smart advisors, she'd built a substantial financial portfolio for herself.

Roger, on the other hand, within a few years of his divorce, had less than half-a-million remaining to his name. Having seen Anna at regular intervals since he'd come to L.A. that summer with Morgenstern, he decided it was time to move in for that crocodile kill and nab her as his next underwriter.

Roger and Anna's first "date" was a workout climbing the hills of Malibu and running on the beach for three miles. He didn't charge her, and took her out to dinner after they'd both showered and cleaned up. Despite his clandestine smoking, steroid and coke habits, the trainer ate a fairly perfect diet to maintain his six-percent body fat and ripped physique. He lived on boiled chicken, salad with no dressing, sweet potatoes and one alcoholic beverage, usually a beer, each week.

How he looked was his calling card, and he'd been doing it for decades by the time he met Anna. Her eating habits were less stellar, but she ate so little, it barely mattered. Anna had grown up associating food with her bloodstained father when he came home at night—sometimes with a slaughtered chicken stuffed into his jacket—and it mostly revolted her. She ate only enough to be able to function and no more.

The trainer had, by this juncture in his life, mastered the art of getting women to do what he wanted without them even realizing it. Once Roger saw Anna's minimalist—but very luxurious—beach house, he knew he had to live there, which motivated him more than anything else to pursue her. She was some 15 years his senior, and while lovely, he was more at home with the large fake breasts and fake tans of women in their thirties who abounded in Hollywood.

But Niles was perfectly capable of forgoing their charms for free rent and the chance to have his training income free and clear for his steroids, drugs, and whatever else he fancied. It wasn't as if Anna was unpleasant to bed, she was simply more delicate and obviously older than what he'd become accustomed to by then.

For the actress, it happened almost imperceptibly, aided by the fact that the mindless sex she shared with Roger opened no locked drawers in her heart or her mind to remind her of her troubled past.

She had never married, despite five proposals over the years and many offers to co-habitate. Anna mostly saw men as a necessary evil, and the idea of emotional connection with one hadn't often entered her mind since she'd left home at 13 that fateful day to escape her father's assaults.

She'd been raped and used so many times by producers and directors and movie stars that she saw it the same way a hooker does: simply as part of her job description. She was mostly numb to what she had been forced to do and had managed to turn it around by embracing sexual pleasure on the occasions when she could find it.

The star simply left her heart out of it, and in Hollywood, so few in the business could get past their own egos that not many sought Anna's heart out: just her body and the chance to brag that they'd bedded her.

It had not even been a year since Anna let Roger move in with her when she first met Dr. Mark Scofield. She was aware that the relationship with her trainer had little substance and truth be told, the sex wasn't even that great. But the Brit did train her for free and he was right there and it was just... easy.

Until she fell for the doctor, she hadn't been able to think of a logical reason to end it. What Anna did know, however, was that she was growing weary of the trainer's frequent rages and insatiable appetite for rough and foreplay-less sex, even if she was less conscious of the cause behind it.

CHAPTER 19

COMING CLEAN

IT HAD CERTAINLY never been Scofield's plan to go public with his budding relationship with Anna, but circumstances were now forcing his hand. Between his P.A. Paul, the very publicly noted emergency room drop off, and now the administered rape kit that might bring up some questions, the doctor realized he was better off coming clean with the police detective squad before they even asked him to come in for questioning.

At least he knew Anna would vouch for him. The rest, he just had to hope would all sound believable, and despite it being completely against medical code, ethics and the law to become involved with a patient, he presumed it would appear less egregious given their mutual ages and elite social statuses in L.A. than if she had been much younger and far less powerful.

Theoretically, the California State Medical Board could take away his license, and at the very least, he would almost certainly be censured, as he was well aware, if the situation became public knowledge, which it now appeared inevitably that it would.

But there was no turning back, nor was he sorry to have gotten involved with his new love, so there it was. Doctors, after all, are human too, and all the training and prohibitions in the world cannot stop two hearts that have found their match.

As a neurosurgeon, Scofield was used to cleaning up messes—caused both by previous surgeons' poor techniques or just anomalies of nature. He knew the best thing to do was to take a moment, devise a game plan, and then proceed step-by-step to make it all come together. He could leave nothing to chance—especially now that he was involved with a major movie star and thus potential gossip fodder for the tabloids. The doctor knew that his very livelihood stood in the balance.

Mark also realized he had to talk to Anna about the whole situation, however painful and uncomfortable that might be for both of them, and voluntarily go in and speak to a detective on the case. Of course, he knew nothing of the actress's sordid past and or how speaking to her might disturb her own nest of buried pain.

Nor did he yet know that Roger had flown the coop and left the country.

It was still only two weeks into Anna's recovery from her spinal fusion, the point at which the pain of spasming muscles tends to reach its apex. The last thing the actress needed right now was more stress, but there was no avoiding it under the circumstances.

Mark had been coming to her house almost nightly, except before surgeries when he needed his sleep. Otherwise, they had sex like two teenagers in the throes of their first love, which, in a sense, it really was for both of them.

⁓

While sex was easy for Anna, human connection was more problematic. She had never had a positive emotional relationship growing up with anyone, and it was like a language she could read, but not entirely understand.

Her feelings for Scofield were so intense, they overwhelmed her at times and made her want to run, but when she saw him, the only place she wanted to run was towards him. He was a lighthouse beacon in a life of nonstop stormy seas, and the only man she had ever been able to sleep with through the night completely peacefully.

Anna wrestled with having found that lighthouse, and her ever-increasing fear that its lights would go out suddenly, or that the entire edifice would crumble and disappear and she would realize it had all only been a dream.

But it is an unusual person who can walk away from a treasure of the heart, let alone such a rare one, and Anna clung to whatever bits of flotsam and jetsam she could find in her own mind to convince herself that she would be alright.

The one thing she did not want to do was share any of her fears with Mark, because she was certain he would leave her if she did. They had shared some pieces of their pasts with each other, but the actress was so used to the fabrications she had created about having been orphaned that she told him this story, even though she was immediately sorry that she had.

Mark had far less to hide, although every human has something they'd rather not reveal early on in a relationship. But Anna's shame was much, much deeper and something she never spoke of to anyone. In a town where going to a shrink was as normal as getting Botox, she had never been to one, afraid if she ever opened that dark and musty box that she would never stop having nightmares.

She learned to change the subject when Scofield probed for more information. Generally, Anna moved to sex, because it was so easy to distract men that way, as well she knew from a lifetime of experience with it. And the sex was so amazing, and sleeping with the doctor so divine—before, during and afterwards—that it was as much for her as it was to keep him off her historical trail.

But for Mark, no such luxury was available when it came time to tell Anna that they would both have to talk to detectives about her attack, and come clean with them about their emerging relationship and how it could impact his surgical practice. While in theory these would be confidential interviews, Scofield knew that every gossip TV show and internet rag in town had moles virtually everywhere who would spill such stories in exchange for confidentiality of their own identities and a fat paycheck.

It is an amazing thing how pleasure of one kind or another can blind members of the human race to its potential consequences. When wrapped in a cocoon of sublime happiness, the ravine towards which we all walk seems so far away, we never imagine having to jump across it, at very peril of our lives. And yet, that day does come.

For Scofield, the precipice was now right in front of him, and the dizzying space into which he could fall was so sobering that for an instant, he may have wished they had never met. Mark knew that the truth would not so much set him free, as forever show him in a different light.

Scofield had called Detective Sandra Locke—whose card he had taken when she came to the hospital to see Anna after the attack by Niles—to arrange a private meeting. He was used to cutting into blood and sinew, muscle and bone, and knew that once that first cut was made, there was nowhere to go but deeper into the flesh, no matter what it looked like or how grotesque its underbelly.

The doctor dressed in a suit to meet Locke at the Santa Monica Metro station. He had cleared his schedule of appointments for the morning, having no idea how long their 9 o'clock interview would last, but he knew there would be many questions. Scofield realized he might even have to give a semen sample at some point, a reality that he did not look forward to.

In the moment when he had to face the repercussions of simply loving someone completely with body, mind and soul, he felt caught in a trap that there was no way out of except to pray for mercy from people who didn't know him or care about his intentions. He had, after all, clearly done something strictly forbidden in medical practice, and that was to become involved sexually and intimately with a patient.

Back in his Harvard Medical School days, he and his class-mates had had discussions about this very issue. They were all in their twenties with raging hormones and had access to end-less naked women willing to disrobe ingenuously before them to be examined on numerous occasions. They were told over and over by professors that this was a sacred trust, and yet they all questioned if not one of these men, throughout their multi-decade careers, had really not a single time taken advantage of these opportunities.

Their discussions back then were less about love and more about lust, of course. What if an attractive woman offered you a blow job while in your office while she had her top off and she had perfect breasts and an exquisite face? To paraphrase Shakespeare, they said, hath not a doctor senses, affections, and passions like any other mortal? Were they to be held to an inhuman standard, rising above it all, no matter how delicious the temptation?

Yes, the elder doctors all told them in class, yes, indeed, they were to rise above it all. But it seemed like a near-impossible task, and at least one fellow classmate later lost his residency at Johns Hopkins when he was found inside a curtained area with an attractive patient down on her knees.

Back then—although Scofield had met more than his share of beauties and certainly could have partaken in any of them—his career goals were sacrosanct and nothing would have come between him and his surgical future. But somehow now, his values had shifted. After all, he had nearly 30 years of being celebrated as the best of the best in his field. What was left to accomplish there?

If it came down to it, he had millions invested in real estate and stock accounts and could retire tomorrow and live comfortably into old age. His values, he realized as he drove the Porsche to the Santa Monica Metro station, had shifted. Time was running out and love was suddenly much more important to him than anything else he could ever experience. His kids were grown and he had never encountered anything when it came to matters of the heart even close to what he felt when he was with Anna.

He wanted to protect her and ravish her all at once, emotions so basic and central to the XY chromosome that they felt exquisitely and perfectly right to him, no matter what consequences they brought.

Scofield pulled into the substation parking lot, put the car in park, and just sat for a moment, closing his eyes. It was as if he knew that when he came back out, he would somehow be a different man in a different position than he was before going in to see the detective.

He pulled down the rearview mirror and straightened his tie. He looked handsome and credible, and he could only hope that Detective Locke had once been—or was still—in love, and would have compassion for him in his very vulnerable professional position.

CHAPTER 20

FACING THE MUSIC

SCOFIELD SAT DOWN in the mirrored interview room inside the Santa Monica substation. It was just him and Detective Locke, but he was well aware that it was mic'd and that he was being recorded both on video and audio.

"I want to thank you for coming in on your own," the detective said, looking at him earnestly. The doctor also knew this was a technique used to win over confidence and make the subject lower their guard. He wanted to tell her to save her time, because he was going to tell her everything he knew anyway, consequences to himself be damned. It was the right thing—and the only thing—to do, when it came down to it, he had decided.

"No problem," Scofield replied, looking back at Locke just as intensely. "I really don't have a ton of information, but I do have some salient facts to share with you that might help your investigation," he said.

"First off—and I'm just going to get this out of the way and into the open right off the bat—Miss Porter and I are involved, romantically speaking. And yes, I know that doing so—not to mention telling you about it—jeopardizes my own medical license or, at the very least, will likely cause the California Medical Board to censure me in some way, but there it is.

"Obviously, it's consensual, but I realize and acknowledge that that is not an excuse, nor does it spare me from whatever punishment may be meted out by the Board."

He stopped to take a breath and a sip of water from the white plastic cup on the desk between them. There, it was done. Nothing else he said after this would be nearly as hard, or as damning.

"I see," Locke said, scribbling some notes on a legal pad. "Well, thank you for your honesty there, Dr. Scofield, I appreciate it. As you said, what the Medical Board does with that information—and you realize I will have to report it to them now—is on them. Is the relationship ongoing and are you still treating her as a physician?"

"Yes and yes," Scofield said softly, lowering his eyes and head. He looked back up and said, "In nearly 30 years in practice, I have never, ever gotten involved with a single patient until now, and that's the truth, you can hook me up to a lie detector test if you want.

"I guess it was just bigger than the both of us. I'd like to tell you I'm sorry it happened, but truthfully, I am not sorry at all. I am very much in love with Miss Porter and I believe she is with me as well."

Locke smiled slightly, in such a way that Scofield couldn't tell if it was sincere or her version of a doctor face. "The heart wants what the heart wants," she said, shrugging and not looking at him, and for a moment, he thought he detected some empathy. But that wouldn't keep her from doing her job and reporting him, and he knew it.

"I feel for you, I really do," she continued. "In this line of work, we see a lot of bad actors, and then we see some people who kind of get caught up in matters that are more of a push against the letter of the law. But we can't ignore that they have broken the law, even though at times – believe me – we wish we could.

"I will have to report this breach to the State Medical Board, and I know you know that, and I applaud your courage and initiative in coming forward of your own volition, and perhaps that will have some effect on their decision regarding how to move forward," Locke said.

"Anyway, now that we have that out of the way, I get the impression that you have more information for me related to this case, is that correct?"

There was a pregnant pause as Scofield looked up at her and took a moment before he said, "Yes, yes, that's right."

"You stay here, I'm going to get us both some coffee," Locke said, standing up and aiming a close-lipped smile towards him. He knew she was going to go discuss what she'd heard so far with her fellow detectives.

"That would be great," the doctor nodded, and leaned back in his chair, exhaling, while she left the room.

Locke came back in with the coffee. Scofield took one sip and put it back down: it was awful and tasted stale. He'd have preferred a swift swig of Scotch at that point, and almost wished he carried a flask of it.

"So," Locke said, looking down at the desk nonchalantly, "tell me what you know about this alleged assault on Miss Porter?"

This was another technique that Scofield was familiar with when it came to law enforcement: after all, he had enough friends who were cops. Ask an open-ended question and see how the interviewee fills in the blanks. His vice squad buddies had regaled him many times with tales of their interviews with perps.

Scofield breathed in deeply and tried to compose himself the way he did before drilling into his patients' spines. He wanted to pick his words carefully.

"I know she had been living with her British personal trainer," he said, pausing before he added, "They were in a relationship of sorts, though not a good one, obviously.

"She called me crying hysterically the morning I rushed her to the hospital, she said something bad had happened between them, but didn't specify what it was. I drove to her house in Malibu and found her collapsed in the hallway and took her to UCLA Santa Monica right away, because she had passed out. I didn't know if he had physically assaulted her, raped her, or both," Scofield said, pausing to look at Locke and make sure she was taking it all in.

"I just wanted to get her medical care, first and foremost. I performed a spinal fusion with laminectomy on her just three weeks ago," he added, realizing as he laid out this story that he was looking like a potential jerk for not only trespassing into the forbidden doctor-patient no-fly zone, but also into the middle of an existing relationship between his now-girlfriend and her then-boyfriend.

"Look, I know I don't exactly look like a prince in this scenario. But I care about Anna deeply and this guy hurt her, clearly. He's taken off to the UK, where he's from, I learned just a few days ago from a friend of his that Anna knows," Mark noted. "Obviously, he was afraid of being charged with assault or rape. As well he probably should be."

Locke was scribbling notes furiously.

"Do you know his name?" she asked.

"Roger Niles," he replied. "I don't know how to find him in Britain, though. I gather his mother still lives there. I think he flew into Heathrow, according to his friend. Honestly, I was kind of glad he was gone and no longer a threat to Anna," Mark said quietly, and Locke realized looking at him that he meant it.

"Ok, thank you, that's all for now," the detective said, standing up. She was tall, and might have been attractive had she not purposefully played down how she looked to be taken seriously in her very male work universe. She wore no makeup and had her bleached blonde hair pulled back into a severe ponytail.

"I have your number, I'll call you if I have any further questions," Locke said as she led him out of the interview room.

CHAPTER 21

UNCHARTED TERRITORY

AS ANNA MOVED into her fourth week of recovery—still in some pain, but moving about more easily—her agent called. Not that Josh Klein hadn't checked in up to that point, but only minimally, so that he could get a sense of how far along she was and how much longer it might be before she would be back up and on the set.

Having never had back surgery himself, Klein thought a month should be more than sufficient time to recover from one, particularly as every day she didn't work, he didn't make his 10 percent.

He'd been Anna's agent for the past 16 years, and knew her foibles and attributes better than almost anyone. The plastic surgery nips and tucks, the bad actors (literally and figuratively) who had come and gone in her life, her finances: he was privy to all of this. Josh had never liked Roger, and had yet to meet Scofield and learn about his unsanctioned connection to Anna when he called.

"Just checking in," he said laconically when Anna answered

her cell. "Wanted to see how you're feeling and if you think you might have a date in mind for when you'll be ready to go back to work. Just a reminder that we only have another month before we are no longer in contract and you can be replaced."

Anna sighed and looked away from the phone. Recovery was hard enough without this pressure, and truthfully, the last thing she wanted to do at that moment was to be on a movie set. She had already heard from Mark about his visit to the detective, and knew that she, too, would have to do an interview soon. Scofield had bought her a little time by saying she was still too fragile to travel much unless it was absolutely necessary.

Anna worried about what it would mean for his career, as he had explained the potential legal and professional repercussions to her. While she'd known it was frowned upon, coming from the movie industry, where there was no sexual guidebook—except the unwritten one that said expect to pay for roles with blow jobs and more if you are a woman—she couldn't conceive of it being such a punitive topic in medicine.

She already felt guilty that she had brought this upon him, and wished—but didn't—that they had never started anything at all. She knew in her heart that to wish such a thing was a lie, because she had never been happier—or felt safer—with a man in her entire life.

Anna worried more that Mark would come to resent her if he was reprimanded by the Medical Board or worse, lost his license to practice entirely. He had assured her he was close to retiring anyway and that her love meant far more to him at this point in his life, but she didn't really believe him, thinking he was saying it just to ease her fears and guilt.

In fact, Scofield meant every word of it, but could never have convinced Anna of that fact.

～

The actress looked back at the phone and cleared her throat. "I'm still in a lot of pain, Josh," she almost whispered, hoping to sound even worse than she felt. "I can't say when, but it won't be this week or next week or probably the week after that. Beyond that, we will just have to see."

Anna knew that before the surgery, she'd have been terrified of losing a role, but now, she almost wished she would. She looked forward to making love with Mark and lying wrapped inside his long, strong arms in bed afterwards, in his enormous terry robe with his initials on it. She needed nothing more to feel completely and totally happy anymore.

She knew all too well that once production on a film started, one's private life went totally to hell, between the brutally long hours on a set, the gossip and backstabbing, and the need to learn lines and practice shoot angles for scenes.

It was why so many actors fell in love with one another while making movies, only to fall out just as quickly once a shoot wrapped: because the make-believe world of Hollywood was so all-encompassing. It left no room for any sense of reality, including meeting anyone not involved in the production.

She could hear her agent's exasperation without him saying a word.

"I'll call you next week with a health update, okay, Josh?" Anna said as reassuringly as possible, hoping to get off the phone quickly. At that moment, she heard Scofield's car pulling up in her driveway and hung up without saying goodbye. Then she rushed to the door to greet him.

Most patients do not have their neurosurgeons show up in the evening with take-out and a passionate kiss. Anna felt like the luckiest woman alive and found the doctor's mix of tenderness and medical concern—combined with his out-and-out unabashed adoration and sexual hunger for her—to be heady stuff indeed.

In fact, Scofield constantly fought the desire to pin her to the wall and fuck her like a whore. He hoped that kind of primal sex would be something to look forward to once she was more healed, but for now, found the softer and more sensual version to be plenty wonderful anyway.

Scofield had been honest with Detective Locke when he said he had never before slept with a patient, not that there hadn't been a few temptations over the years. But he had always managed to resist women who had thrown themselves at him in his office before Anna. He had to admit it felt amazing to succumb at last, with a woman as exquisite as the actress, no less.

Sometimes successful doctor Mark would think back on his 20-something resident self at Johns Hopkins, and ponder with amazement that he was now the real-life love interest of the actress he had been so attracted to when she appeared on screen in her major starring roles almost 30 years before.

❧

Anna had, by now, told him what happened that dark night with Roger. He stroked her hair while she relayed the whole episode to him and wiped away her tears. It pained him to see her so fragile that she seemed almost like she could break in two. And he was glad that Niles had crossed the pond and was out of his reach.

What Anna hadn't yet revealed to him was her even more troubling childhood. She wanted to very badly, but her absolute terror of losing him if she told him her father had repeatedly raped her as a young girl held her back. She knew intuitively that most men would find that a revolting thought and would see her as spoiled goods, or worse.

But that night, after making love—and as Mark sipped his Scotch—she somehow found the courage at last to broach the subject with him. After all, he had risked everything for her, telling the cops about their relationship. Surely, Anna owed him something equally terrifying that came from her own soul. She gazed up into his eyes from where she lay curled against his strong chest, and then turned slightly, still wincing in pain.

"I have to tell you something," she whispered, and he pulled her in closer. He absolutely loved anything that would unravel the mystery about her, but knew if he pushed too hard for information, she would retreat like a turtle into her shell.

"Tell me anything, baby doll," the doctor said, his arm wrapped around her like a fortress that could not be invaded.

There was a long pause as Anna lowered her head, that feeling of being dirty and shameful sweeping over her, as her tears fell like a summer monsoon.

"My father… I've never told anyone this," she said, looking up at him in a way so vulnerable that it made him feel even more powerful. "He raped me," she said in the softest voice possible. "Not once, I mean, many, many times, when I was a pre-teen. Probably hundreds of times. He worked on a chicken farm and he smelled disgusting and my mother wouldn't sleep with him so he would come into my room and do whatever he wanted and that's why I ran away at 13 and came to Hollywood and probably another couple hundred men have raped me since," she blurted out, fully sobbing now, so hard that she could hardly speak.

Scofield didn't say anything, not because he was horrified or even, somehow, surprised, but because there seemed to be no words that could convey the sorrow and anger he felt that she had been so abused for so many years by so many men, let alone her father.

"Honey, come here," he said, pulling her in as close as he could. "I love you—and nothing that's happened to you makes any difference to me. I am so sorry that you had to suffer like that, baby girl. You didn't deserve any of it, and no man will ever hurt you again as long as I'm around to stop them," he added, stroking her long loose hair repeatedly as she cried.

She felt free for the first time in her life, her secret finally revealed. And she hadn't even been swallowed up into the Earth, as she'd always feared would happen if she ever told the truth about her childhood to anyone.

CHAPTER 22

LOCKED UP IN MALIBU

IN THE END, Detective Sandra Locke came down to see Anna in her Malibu beach house, because Scofield didn't want her sitting on hard police station chairs as she recovered—or being set off emotionally in that environment. He knew it was hard enough for his girlfriend to talk about any of it.

Locke had dealt with her fair share of rapes and assaults and knew that living in the better hoods of Los Angeles was no protection from their occurrence. She was sensitive to the issues that the doctor had skirted around in asking her to question Anna gently, and knew all about family patterns of violence, having come from such a background herself.

Anna asked the detective if she wanted coffee or tea, but Locke politely refused, taking out her large legal pad and a ballpoint pen and settling down on the crisp white linen sofa. Locke had noticed over the years that wealthy celebrities liked white furnishings, as if to say, "I can afford cleaning people if you spill red wine on this."

"May I ask what your relationship was with your attacker?" Locke said quietly, pen poised.

"He was living with me," Anna responded with her head down. "I guess you could say we were involved, though it sounds revolting to me now," she added.

The detective nodded. "I understand," she said, pausing before she said, "And what is his name?"

"Roger Niles," Anna told her. "He's back in the UK now with his mother, from what I understand. I've had no communication with him, of course. I just asked a friend of his that I know a bit, we dropped all of his belongings over there, too. He didn't tell us much. To be honest, I don't think he really knew that much himself, just that Roger had fled the country after he assaulted me, which should tell you that he knew that what he did was very wrong."

Locke leaned in towards Anna and reached out a hand to take the actress's tiny one. "Sometimes us mere mortals forget that you movie stars are also human," she said earnestly. "You're not the first famous celebrity who's been sexually assaulted, believe me. And I've seen first-hand the toll it can take.

"I hope you will reach out for help or counseling, it's out there, and it will stay confidential. I wouldn't want you to be scarred by this," the detective added, leaning back again and taking her hand away from the star's.

Anna was somewhat emboldened from her recent revelations to Mark and how kindly they had been received, and suddenly didn't care who knew what about her. Maybe it would help some other woman who was in the same boat she had once been in, she thought, imagining that somehow whatever she shared with the detective would be leaked to the media, as always seemed to happen in these scandalous scenarios in Hollywood.

"It's not the first time I've been raped," she almost whispered, her head lowered again, but looking up at Locke. "I was raped often as a young girl by my own father, and in this industry…," her voice trailed off for a moment as she looked towards the Pacific, lapping against the private beach outside, with its waves that had drowned out her bad childhood memories for so many years.

"Well, it happens a lot, as I'm sure you know. Not now, at this stage of my career, but when I started out, I was 13, so…," she stopped, looking for any trace of shock in the detective's countenance.

But there was none to be found.

CHAPTER 23

JUDGMENT DAY

BACK DURING SCOFIELD'S days at Harvard and Johns Hopkins, the prohibition against getting involved with patients made at least some sense to him. And the doctor still understood its purpose when it came to caring for under-aged, mentally challenged, or otherwise less-than-equal persons who could not honestly assess whether being in such a relationship was a wise move for them.

But at 59—in love with a woman four years his senior—and both of them having had enough worldly experience to fill several football fields, the hard-and-fast rule struck him as utterly absurd. After all, didn't bosses marry their secretaries all the time? No one was arresting them or taking away their business licenses for doing so.

Scofield found himself resenting the fact that, because of a few bad apples, the entire medical community now faced these rigid rules that turned the ecstasy of love and meeting your soulmate into a shameful—and even possibly criminal—act.

He'd been called in front of the California Medical Board

after Detective Locke filed her report to them. She really believed that Scofield and Anna were the exception that proved the rule, but the law was the law was the law, and that was that. She had no choice but to let the Board know.

He'd considered getting an attorney to face what amounted to a court trial with an Administrative Law Judge presiding, who would then present his recommendation to the 15-member Board. They would have the authority to do as they wished, and could choose to enforce, modify, or entirely reject the recommendation, at their discretion.

In the end, Scofield decided—despite the old adage that a man who represents himself has a fool for a client—that just being honest and forthright was his best approach. He had no intention of being contrite, especially since he was both still technically Anna's neurosurgeon as well as her lover, and wasn't planning on letting either role go.

He entered the administrative hearing wearing a dark and serious-looking suit. Anna had wanted to come, but these were closed proceedings, not open to the public like a regular criminal trial, and he also thought she might be a distraction to any decision-makers. He'd promised to call her as soon as the hearing wrapped up.

The doctor faced the judge in the small court room and stood up as the charge was read. In his mind, he was thinking, "Yes, I'm in love with a patient, guilty as charged, Your Honor," but he stood silent and stone-faced instead.

"Dr. Mark Scofield," the judge began, his voice low and bellowing as he read the page in front of him. "According to the California Medical Board Business and Professions Code section 726, which states that 'sexual abuse, misconduct or relations with a patient are considered unprofessional... and grounds for disciplinary action,' you have been brought to this hearing to answer these charges.

"The Board's Code section 726 further states that 'any type of personal relationship between the doctor and the patient [is] a very serious breach of public trust,' and a matter to be considered for censure or license suspension. Do you have legal counsel with you today?"

"No, Your Honor, I am here representing myself, and will speak for myself," Scofield said, lowering his head to show deference and respect to the judge, who sighed, having seen such foolish choices too many times over his nearly 40 years on the bench.

"Very well, Dr. Scofield," the judge said, looking straight at him. "And how do you plead?"

"Your Honor, I plead technically guilty, but with an explanation," Scofield said, knowing full well this was not an option when pleading. But he had nothing more to lose at this point.

"Miss Porter and I are very much in love and we are both well into our lives with expansive experiences behind us and feel that who we choose to spend time with at this juncture should really be an entirely personal matter and not one for a court of law or a medical board to determine," Scofield said calmly. He'd practiced saying it at least 10 times in front of his mirror at home.

The judge leaned forward and took his spectacles off as he addressed Mark.

"Dr. Scofield, I am sure you are aware—and I quote from the Code—that 'the fact that the personal relationship between the physician and the patient at some point was consensual does not negate the fact that the physician breached professional ethics and boundaries, and possibly broke the law, by initiating a personal relationship with a patient,'" the judge said harshly.

"You are and were aware of this reality when you started seeing Miss Porter, were you not?"

"I am and I was, Your Honor," the doctor said quietly. "I was absolutely aware that it was against everything I had always learned about being a medical professional. But there are times in life when rules must be broken to avoid losing something so precious and amazing that to let it slip away would be the worst decision of your life," he added.

"My feelings for Miss Porter are of that magnitude, and the fact that we met in my medical office was perhaps unfortunate, but she needed a spinal fusion and that's what I do. And once having met in this setting—and feeling such an enormous pull towards one another—we couldn't undo where we'd met, and we wanted to be together, and we are both hovering around 60 years old, and I find myself struggling to find why I must apologize, being a divorced man, for loving a single woman who is close to my age and who I find beautiful in every way that a man can find a woman attractive.

"So, if you must sanction me, Your Honor, or recommend to the Medical Board that they do so at your behest, or if you must take away my license, then please, just get it over with, and let's not waste each other's time," Scofield said, almost out of breath by this point.

There was total silence in the tiny courtroom as the judge leaned back in his huge chair and sucked on the end of his glasses for a minute, all the while staring at Scofield in amazement.

"Well, that was quite a speech, Doctor," the judge said. "And as a man and as a human being, I do empathize with you and have compassion for your plight. But as a judge—in which role I appear here today—I must weigh the facts of the case and make my recommendation to the Medical Board based on that, and that alone.

"And on that basis, I have to find you guilty of breaching the Business and Professions Code section 726 with an inappropriate personal and sexual relationship with a patient who is still in your care," the judge said, pausing to let the gravity of it all sink in.

"I do cut you some slack for your mutual years and for the fact that you are both single and well over the age of majority, but I cannot in good faith cut you much more than that on that front. So, while I will not recommend that the Board take away your license to practice, I will recommend that you be forced to either cease to treat Miss Porter as your patient, or cease seeing her as your girlfriend, or both.

"Additionally," the judge continued, "I will recommend that you take a forced sabbatical from practice for a period of not less than six months, after which, you may resume practice with the understanding that should this ever happen again with anyone else for any reason, you will lose your right to practice medicine once and for all. Do I make myself clear, Doctor Scofield?"

"Yes, Your Honor, perfectly so," Scofield almost whispered back, his head once more bowed.

❧

It was a month before the doctor received the Medical Board's final decision by mail. By this point, it had been two months since he'd performed Anna's surgery. Her pain had finally broken and she was starting to move around more easily without having to down muscle relaxers and Tylenol every day.

Anna saw the letter first. She was waiting for him at his home in a silky robe and negligee on the day it arrived. He'd given her a key to his house several weeks earlier and was always happy to find her there when he came back from surgeries.

He was so in love with her that it was like a soft cloud of happiness that followed him everywhere. If Anna had met her counterpart in his physical and mental strength and calm demeanor, he'd met his with the actress's vulnerable beauty. He needed to feel needed, and Anna made him feel like the most important man who'd ever lived, because to her, he was exactly that.

The letter was clearly several pages—Anna could tell just holding the envelope—and she knew her lover's future was outlined in it. She left it on top of his mail pile, poured herself a glass of iced tea, and stepped out onto the second-floor balcony that overlooked the city below and the ocean a few miles away. It didn't have the lapping waves of her beachfront home, but it was a beautifully manicured, well-appointed two-story that showcased the doctor's success nonetheless.

She felt protected at his house, even when he wasn't there. It was secluded, with its surrounding landscaping and over an acre of land to buffer the lavish Mediterranean-style villa. When Anna saw Mark's Porsche pull up to the three-car driveway below the terrace, she turned and quickly went downstairs.

She threw her arms around his neck that was a good foot above her own, and he picked her up from under her butt and easily twirled her around while she sank into him. His smell was so divine to her that she could have just breathed him for hours: it had an aura of safety and sanity and sexiness all rolled into one.

But on the third twirl, he spotted the letter out of the corner of his eye, and slowly put Anna back down as he reached over for it. She watched his face with worry, wondering what lay inside and what it would mean for them and their future.

Mark held the letter for a moment, unopened, and then walked over to his bar and poured himself a Scotch on ice. He knew his life was about to change and he wanted to get some liquid courage before he found out his fate.

Scofield sat down on the big soft sofa, and patted his lap for Anna to sit on, which she always happily did. Coming from a family that was not only abusive and neglectful, but also emotionally frigid, she found his desire for nearly constant physical closeness to be a small slice of heaven. Mark had never really explained to her how barren his own childhood had been, and how she equally compensated him for all those years of emptiness.

With Anna's hair and robe pressed against his chest and his tie loosened, Scofield took a large swig of whiskey and then opened the letter and unfolded its thick parchment-like paper.

Doctor Scofield:

In light of the recommendation of Judge Stanley Korwith regarding the charges of inappropriate sexual behavior with a patient and your own admission of guilt in this matter, we hereby have determined the following shall be our course of action:

1. *You will suspend all surgical activities for a period of not less than six months, commencing immediately, and will have all your patients who need follow-up care referred to professionals you know and respect during that time. It will be up to you what reason you give your patients for this turn of events.*

2. *During this time off, you will take a required two-month course in appropriate sexual behavior between doctors and patients. While you may complete this course online, the Board will have strict guidelines for you to prove that you have taken such a course and you will have to pass a written test on the subject matter upon its completion.*

3. *If numbers 1) and 2) are fulfilled to the Board's satisfaction, you will come before us on a mutually agreed-upon date and we will determine if we feel you are fit to return to private practice.*

Please sign and return the attached, signifying that you understand this course of censure and will abide by it to the letter, at which time we will coordinate the details that will need to be presented to us to ensure that you are taking this matter seriously.

After much consideration, the Board has determined that no criminal charges will be filed against you.

Sincerely yours,

Carlton P. Patel, M.D., President
California Medical Board

Scofield slowly folded the letter back up and slid it into its envelope. There was plenty of time to consider its ramifications later. It was Friday night, and all he wanted to do was make love to Anna.

CHAPTER 24

NEW DIRECTIONS

FOR MARK, THAT letter was the end of the road, and he knew he only had one choice: to completely change his course.

After dedicating his life to helping patients regain mobility, he suddenly realized he had perhaps been losing his own. He no longer wanted the State Medical Board and the whims of its 15 members to determine his lifestyle choices. Scofield had never felt righter about anything than he did about being with Anna Porter, and he was damned if was going to let the California Board turn his pure and sacred love into something dirty and perverted.

After making French toast on Saturday morning for Anna—who he'd quickly learned did not count cooking among her many skills—the doctor had reopened the letter and read it through slowly at least five times as he sipped dark roast coffee from a huge mug. Anna watched his face intently, wondering what he was thinking.

He finally looked up and smiled at her.

"I'm going to sell my practice, babe," he said definitively, slapping the table. "You're almost healed anyway, and I'd rather go out on a high note than have to grovel to these doctors."

"Is this really what you want to do?" Anna said, pulling her chair close to his. "Will you be happy? I don't ever want you to resent me," she said, looking searchingly at his face for any trace that he might. She felt if she lost Mark now, her life would have no meaning ever again.

The doctor put his hand under her chin and lifted her head to look straight into her eyes, those eyes that still made him melt every time he looked at them.

"Anna, listen to me," he said. "Not only will I never resent you, you're the greatest gift that's ever come into my life." The actress couldn't have felt more adored if she'd been handed an Oscar at the Academy Awards in front of millions of fans. She smiled slowly at him, and he grinned back.

"I can't keep doing this work much longer anyway, it's physically and mentally draining and I'd be retiring within the next few years regardless. I have plenty of money and can probably make several million more selling the practice. It won't happen overnight, but it's the right move and frees me from having to cater to the medical board," he added.

"But what will you do all day?" Anna asked earnestly. She herself knew a call was coming shortly from her agent about the movie and her ability to return to work, a prospect she wasn't looking forward to at all. She'd been in a cocoon of sorts these past two months. The thought of going back to a set felt like falling into a black hole filled with snakes, and she dreaded it.

"Let's travel," Scofield said, pulling her face close to his and searching it for approval. "We have enough money, between the two of us, to live a good life for decades to come, if we live that long," he said.

Anna said nothing and just studied his face to make sure he was serious.

"I don't mind giving up the movie business at all," she said softly, and laid her head into his neck as she breathed in his scent. His hand stroked her hair and he kissed the top of her head.

"It's a chance for both of us to start a new chapter, babe," he whispered into her ear, and she nestled even closer to him, kissing his chest.

"I hate making movies. I hate Hollywood, it's just all I've ever known," she said. "I would rather be with you than anything else in the world." And with that, Mark picked her up and carried her upstairs.

∽

Josh Klein was mostly a patient man: he had to be to deal with his Hollywood clientele. But Anna Porter had now passed the two-month mark, which meant that she could be released from her upcoming role in "Honor Guard"—a film about Marines who guarded the White House and the drama in their home lives—at any time. She was playing the mother of one of those soldiers, whose own husband had been an elite US commando killed in Afghanistan.

It was a great role for the star, and more than a cameo, which for a woman in her 60s in Hollywood was no small thing. Klein had negotiated a nice payday for Anna, promising that she would do the talk show circuit and present at the panoply of award shows that started in February each year in L.A. Designers loved to dress her size-two frame, and she was as telegenic as they came, even in a closeup, and even at her age.

She was the older woman that younger guys wanted to bed, and that women in her demographic wished they could look like. Because of that, she had a potential cosmetics contract in the works, since her fans were willing to spend almost anything to stay attractive and she was aspirational for them. Even a major pharmaceutical company had approached Klein to open a dialogue about using her to shill for their anti-aging products in TV spots and at some major convention appearances, and these were for some serious promotional fees.

Klein himself was 46, and had been with Anna since he hit 30 as her agent. She was far from his most difficult client, though she did require some coddling and at times needed to be bolstered up, but who in Hollywood didn't? The glamourous façade that most actresses of any age presented on the red carpet was mostly just that, and usually hid a mass of insecurities and abandonment issues that were stuffed away under near-starvation and grueling workouts with harsh personal trainers like Roger Niles.

Klein had already decided to visit Anna in person at her home, and he planned to do it when the doctor—who seemed, to the annoyed agent, to have taken her over, body and soul—wasn't around. He had to convince her to get back in the saddle and back to work.

He knew she was physically able to now, but she seemed to have come up with a million excuses why she wasn't ready to return to the set. Time was running out if Anna wanted to keep this role, and if she lost it, it wouldn't help her already limited movie career options, as Klein was only too aware.

The agent had negotiated a seven-figure payday for his client, and 10 percent of $1,200,000 for three weeks of work and a media tour was $120,000 he wasn't prepared to lose. A thin, unflamboyant gay man with a small goatee, Klein drove down the Malibu canyon mapping out his plan of attack in his mind.

He knew the best way to convince Anna to get back to work was by waving dollar signs in front of her face: she had grown up poor and money had always meant a great deal to her. He would reiterate not only her extravagant fee for this minimal amount of work, but all the commercial deals that hung in the balance afterwards that were even more money for even less work.

Not to mention that all of it kept her relevant to her fan base.

⁓

Klein pulled up to Anna's house in his dark blue Mercedes convertible, and sat for a moment in the large driveway to compose his thoughts. He planned to leave with a commitment from the actress to return to work within days and complete her contract on the film.

He walked up the steps to her house and rang the bell, hearing the ocean on the other side as he waited. Anna opened the door looking wonderful. She was rested and happy. Her hair was pulled up into a messy bun and her white cotton A-line dress accentuated her tiny waist. She smiled broadly at him and gestured for him to come in. It was mid-afternoon and the sun was already coming over the ocean side of the house with its warm golden glow.

Anna sipped herbal tea with her bare feet tucked to the side on the white sofa. She offered Josh the same—or a cocktail or wine—but he passed and opened his briefcase to talk business.

"You know we're already a week past the point where they can recast you with no consequences," he said, looking at the star earnestly. "Fortunately, they haven't exercised that option, and if I can give them a start date that's in the near future, I don't think they will. It's only a three-week shoot commitment and the only travel will be for promotion after it comes out, which is at least a few months away, so you'll have more than enough time to continue healing before that hectic pace kicks in.

"I get that you enjoy spending time with your doctor. But this is a heck of a piece of business and several very lucrative commercial contracts also ride in the balance, so we really shouldn't let this opportunity pass, Anna," Klein said, somewhat sternly.

He paused to let the gravity of the situation sink in as he stared at the actress intently.

"$1.2 mil for three weeks' work, and another possible couple mil for TV spots, appearances, and conventions," he said quietly. "Frankly, you'd be damned foolish to let this situation slip away, Anna, and as your agent, it's my job to make sure you do not make foolish career choices."

The actress leaned back on the sofa and looked out towards the ocean. She had so enjoyed the pressure-less few months of recovery from her spinal fusion, even though she'd endured so much pain to get there. It was a break she had never taken since she'd landed in Hollywood half a century before.

But if she and Mark were going to retire and travel the world together—and it would take him a bit of time to get his practice sold—she might as well go for one last hurrah in show business and make some money doing it, she realized. Anna was almost afraid to stop working, lest she somehow discover it was now midnight and her coach and four would be turning back into a pumpkin and some field mice before she could make it home.

"Anna?" Josh asked, leaning in. "Are you with me? What do you say? Can I give the producers a definite date for your return to the set?"

The professional in her suddenly took over as Porter

dropped her feet to the fuzzy white throw carpet and smiled at her agent.

"Yes," she said, "yes, I am in. Tell them I will be back on the set come next Monday and get me a call time and a script."

CHAPTER 25

QUIET ON THE SET

ANNA'S FIRST DAY back at work was a shock to her system. After so many weeks of being able to relax in Mark's enormous terry robe and just watch the waves and smell the salt water uninterrupted, the massive machine that is a Hollywood movie set was like hitting midtown Manhattan at rush hour after driving backwoods country roads in the South for a month.

Truth be told, the producers and director were glad they would not have to recast Anna's part, as they considered her a perfect fit for it. And one thing the actress had earned in her many years in the business was a reputation for being a reliable and hard worker who always showed up on time. And time, after all, was money in the movie industry.

Anna entered her trailer and took stock of its interior. It looked like one of those models they show at conventions: fully tricked out, but completely lacking in anything that could be considered vaguely eccentric or personal.

Not knowing if she would be back, the producers hadn't

paid much attention to the usual contractual addendums that demand certain kinds of flowers, minimum thread counts on sheets, or insanely expensive bottled water brands. Still, the trailer was ready and waiting for her and it was clean.

⁓

Scofield hadn't been thrilled to hear she was going back to the film after all. Less than the three weeks of work it entailed, the doctor wondered what a cross-country media tour would entail, and if she would suddenly realize she wasn't ready to get out of show business after all.

But he hadn't risen to the top of the most elite field in medicine by being paranoid or suspicious, so he set his fears aside and told her to do whatever she needed to do to be happy. He knew he would pursue Anna wherever she went on Earth, and he had no intention of losing her to some smooth-talking actor who might be 20 years his junior, no matter what moves they made.

⁓

People in love waiver madly between euphoria and terror, often several times a day. The very thing that elates them also puts them on a precipice from which to fall: those alluring words "I'm in love with you" create a cliff and a ravine where none stood before. Suddenly, the need to protect this new-found escarpment becomes critical.

Such was the case for Scofield, who had forgotten how it felt to be in love and feel loved until he met Anna, and who would now rather lose his right hand than such an intoxicating sensation. He would wake up in the middle of night and watch her sleep, so petite, her hair sprawled on his pillow, her lips curled into a soft smile that he knew he had put there just hours before. Sometimes he would stroke her hair as she adjusted slightly, and maybe awoke for a second to move closer to him, and he would wrap himself around her and take her in like a thirsty man in the desert drinks from a fresh well. She had become sustenance for his soul now, and he could never let her get away.

⁓

Anna, meanwhile, showed up at 5 a.m. for her makeup and wardrobe fittings that first Monday back. The character she was portraying was considerably more shopworn than the actress herself, living in a trailer in the South, and makeup had to give the actress the subtle appearance of a more faded beauty than she actually possessed. They gave her a wig with slight gray roots and a tacky shade of red, and it looked—as on set hair and makeup must—alarmingly real once in place.

She suddenly thought, looking in the mirror, that this was how she would likely have looked now if she wasn't living in Hollywood and hadn't had a few lifts and tweaks over the years, along with ongoing fillers and Botox to maintain her appearance.

By seven o'clock, the assistant director came for her, and Anna carried her script, still memorizing her fairly short interchange with Tom Madison, the roughly handsome actor in his late thirties who played her grown son.

Anna had seen him at awards shows, but had never met Madison before, and was struck by his searing blue eyes inside a real tan and a ripped physique. Even in love, one can still admire the pulchritude of a member of the opposite sex for a fleeting moment. But her own man was in amazing shape and fulfilled every fantasy she could have ever dreamed of, leaving her with no more than a small zap of sexual attention for anyone else.

"QUIET ON THE SET," the AD yelled, hitting the clapperboard together, as Anna and Tom began their dialogue.

∼

The shoot went quickly enough, after which Anna and Mark had six months off together before her cross-country media tour kicked off.

Scofield had talked to his partners about buying him out of the practice, and everyone agreed it would be the best course of action for all involved. The last thing his fellow practitioners wanted, after all, was a scandal to mar the group's reputation.

All that remained was for his lawyers to draw up the terms and for everyone to agree on what they were. Scofield knew he would get the short end of the stick: after all, the sale was because of his poor decisions from a professional standpoint, even if he thought the entire situation was ridiculous.

He hoped to have at least the majority of the terms decided before Anna went on tour, as he knew he would be distracted by her absence. She'd become an emotional anchor for him, and what he most looked forward to on any given day. The thought of her being gone for even a few weeks left a hole in the pit of his stomach.

He'd visited the set just one time, when Anna had asked Mark if he wanted to see how movies were made. He entered her private high-end trailer and shook hands with her co-star Tom Madison and immediately felt something he seldom had in his nearly 60 years on the planet: jealousy. The actor was a classic ladies' man heartthrob type, with a dimple and a smile that would melt butter, and Scofield perceived him as a threat.

Even when Anna assured him she had no interest and that

her co-star typically went for 20-something starlets, the doctor still fought his own uneasiness over how much time the duo would be spending together each day on the set.

So when the shoot wrapped, Scofield exhaled a sigh of relief. He suddenly realized why so few Hollywood marriages ever survived more than a few years, as who could resist the endless stream of eye candy from both sexes?

It was during the shoot that Mark—perhaps spurred on by a fear of losing her—decided he would seal the deal and propose to Anna. Marriage wasn't anything they'd formally discussed, but the doctor wanted to show her that he intended to stand by her forever. He realized that while she was away would be a perfect time to ring shop without her getting wind of it, which would at least distract him somewhat from her temporary absence while the actress did her media tour duties.

Mark had done some initial looking in jewelry stores around town, and knew Anna well enough by now to know she would want something delicate and unique over huge and flashy. After all, they weren't kids trying to impress each other with how much money they could spend. But he wanted the ring to be custom-made and have the best quality center-stone diamond, and those, he well knew, didn't come cheap.

Klein had coordinated with the film's marketing team about which cities Anna would fly to, in what order, and what local and national appearances she would make along the way to promote "Honor Guard," which they planned to release in time for Christmas. From L.A., she would fly to San Diego, then Phoenix, Houston, Chicago, and Philadelphia, finally ending up in New York for the grand slam of appearances on all the major networks and at a few preview parties for critics.

She'd be in Manhattan for three days doing appearances and social events, while the other cities were spread over a total of eight days, including flights.

Scofield found her itinerary and booked himself into the same high-end hotel near Central Park in Manhattan where Anna had reservations. He decided to keep it a surprise, along with when and where he would propose to her.

The doctor went into Harry Winston on Rodeo Drive one day after work. He'd called and they'd promised to let him in after hours on a Monday, knowing that a successful neurosurgeon was likely to drop some serious change on an engagement ring. Anna's hands were so tiny, and he knew she wore a size 4½ on her ring finger, having measured one from her jewelry box when she was soaking in a bath one evening.

He pictured a 3 ½ carat near-flawless center stone and a baguette-encrusted platinum band. By Hollywood standards, that was understated. For the quality of stone Mark wanted and the custom design and extra diamonds—not to mention the Harry Winston name—he was looking at about $125,000 for Anna's proposal jewelry.

The manager brought out three round center stone options of the quality and carat weight Mark wanted, and let the doctor look at them through a jeweler's loop. Scofield was no diamond expert, but picked a near-colorless one that was both dazzling, and, as it turned out, the most expensive of the three.

An in-house designer then drew up a sketch and showed the doctor the delicate setting of baguette stones that would sit on the front of the platinum band, promising a 10-day turnaround. Scofield hadn't expected to ever marry again, and the ease with which he was moving forward surprised even himself. But it all felt as right as anything he'd ever done in his life.

⁓

Anna's stylist helped her pack for the junket. Every stop had its own wardrobe coordinated with shoes and jewelry, and a hair and makeup person would accompany her on the entire trip. Although morning interview shows had their own people to do such things on set, the film's producers didn't mind spending the money to make sure the star looked and felt her best on the tour.

The actress had done dozens of these junkets over the years and was at ease in front of a camera, even showing an otherwise largely hidden comedic streak when she was on talk shows. Besides Ed Sullivan and Jackie Gleason, she'd grown up watching celebrities on "The Tonight Show" being interviewed by then-host Johnny Carson and his sidekick Ed McMahon, and the duo were arguably the masters of the comedic closeup deadpan face. She'd absorbed it without even knowing how, and put her own version of the silently expressive comedy take to use when it suited her.

The tours were exhausting, with virtually every minute mapped out, and Anna had handlers and PR people and stylists all keeping her afloat. It was several TV interviews per city, followed by print and digital pressers, and then onto the airport and the next flight and the next city to do it all over again. It quickly became hard to remember what had already been said and to whom and not to repeat oneself and sound canned.

By Day Seven, when the entire crew landed at JFK in New York, everyone was exhausted. But it was also the city where the media impact—nationally and internationally—was the greatest, so that last marathon push of energy was critical.

Anna checked into the Essex House on Central Park South, where she always stayed in the city. It was an area that had been very exclusive—and impossibly chic—until sometime in the 1990s, when the bougie Russian, Chinese, and Middle Eastern billionaires started to infiltrate the area with their all-cash purchases of co-ops and high rises in midtown Manhattan.

Over the past 10 years, the ever-escalating tourist trade around the entrance to the park that stood directly opposite the hotel had also been permeated by dozens of foreigners—hawking bicycles for rent and carriage tours—making it almost impossible to walk unaccosted on that side of the street.

On top of that, scaffolding was everywhere, as developers tried to modernize the old skyscrapers that had been built close to 100 years prior. Even worse, efforts at minimizing the ugliness of the ubiquitous metal rods and wooden planks simply made it look tackier, with fake boxwood plant hedges laid over the makeshift rods.

Once inside, the age of the building showed in spots, although the guest rooms had, of course, been remodeled numerous times over the years. Anna had a suite with a small terrace and a park view.

At least she knew the end—and a chance to see Mark again—was near. They'd facetimed, but it wasn't nearly the same as breathing in his manliness and feeling it inside her, and she missed laying in his protective arms at night, where she slept better than she ever had in her entire life.

CHAPTER 26

CHATTING IT UP

ANNA ENTERED THE ABC headquarters building on West 66th in Manhattan—about ten blocks from her hotel—with her publicist and hair and makeup team in tow. She was going to be interviewed on "Good Morning America" about "Honor Guard," and had her spiel pretty much down pat by this juncture in the press tour.

She sat down in makeup with a robe around her outfit and a shoulder paper wrap that looked like a lobster bib for a pilgrim, designed to keep powder from falling on her clothes. Her girls opened their monster fishing tackle boxes—so big they had their own wheels so no one pulled a shoulder out of its socket hauling them—and got to work on her still-bare face and hair.

"30 minutes, Miss Porter," an assistant director said, poking his head in and disappearing just as quickly. Anna sipped coffee from a plastic mug with a straw, so as to minimally impact her lipstick.

TV makeup is different than that used in real life, as it has to withstand the washout from hundreds of overhead

Klieg lights that create the near-flawless look of all network anchors everywhere.

So Anna let them pancake her foundation on and over-emphasize her eyes in a way that she knew Mark would hate. Bright red lip gloss finished it off, as her hair was teased into a high and intentionally messy updo, and that was it for the coffee with the straw until the segment was over.

She waited for the AD to return about three minutes before her segment to lead her down the cement corridors that all TV stations everywhere have, to the "ON AIR" doors where she would wait to be introduced to the small studio audience.

"Ok, you're on!" the AD whispered, listening to the anchor via his headset, and pushed her through the doors to the brightly lit set.

⁓

Scofield had taken the Jet Blue red eye from LAX into JFK, hoping to surprise Anna at her hotel after the junket was wrapped for the day. He'd already arranged with security how he would show up at Anna's hotel room.

He had the $125,000 diamond-and-platinum ring carefully nestled in a lavish jewelry box sitting in his inside jacket pocket.

Scofield had booked a first-class seat and boarded the Airbus A321 right after the wheelchairs, babies and veterans. A flight attendant offered him a glass of champagne, which he happily accepted. In approximately 6 ½ hours, he would be deplaning, taking a reserved limo into Manhattan, and getting showered, shaved and changed to meet Anna at the hotel, unbeknownst to her, of course.

He sipped the champagne slowly and smiled thinking about being with her. Two weeks had seemed like two years to the doctor, and fucking her every way he could imagine was his top priority.

He still hadn't decided exactly when or where the proposal would take place. The doctor closed his eyes as the plane took off and napped the entire flight.

~~∕∕∕~~

Anna returned to the Essex House in the late morning and took a long nap before washing off all of the TV makeup, and what seemed like a can of spray from her hair. She wrapped herself in Mark's robe, breathing in his scent from the neck as if it were the most expensive French perfume.

He'd told her he would be with his lawyers all day so that she wouldn't try to text him and wonder why he didn't respond. Her stylists were to keep her in her room until he got there. As far as Anna knew, the crew was having a quiet meal downstairs in the hotel restaurant before their very early morning flight back to LAX, for which they would be leaving en masse for JFK at 3 a.m.

Mark had already showered and shaved in his room, and had security on alert for his carefully crafted plan. He put on an expensive dark suit that he knew Anna loved when he'd worn it in L.A., and slapped on just enough of her favorite cologne to wake up her animal appetites. His needed no awakening, that was for sure: he had to fight his erection constantly whenever he thought about doing her again.

He called her stylists to find out if she was in her room. After checking that she was, they offered to come help her do hair and makeup for dinner that night. When they left, with Anna looking naturally lovely and her hair swept up in a much softer and less teased and sprayed version of that morning's messy updo, they texted Mark to let him know it was all clear for him to make his move.

He called down to security and told them to make their call. Anna answered the room phone, unsure who would be calling her on it.

"Miss Porter, this is Victor Estevez in maintenance, we need to access your room briefly if this is a good time. Just a minor electrical issue that we traced back to your room and we want to fix it quickly for you, if that's ok."

Anna was perplexed, as everything seemed to be working fine, but agreed to let maintenance come by to fix the issue, whatever it was.

Within 10 minutes, the doorbell rang. "Miss Porter, it's Victor Estevez in maintenance, may I enter?" he bellowed right outside her room, with Mark Scofield standing by his side and adjusting his tie nervously.

Anna pulled her huge shapeless robe closer around her, knowing her tiny frame was completely naked underneath. She pulled open the door and saw Mark holding a bouquet of roses and a grin the size of Montana. The maintenance guy was already long gone down the hallway.

∽

Mark's smile grew bigger as he saw the look of amazement on her face. He pushed the heavy door closed, dropped the flowers on the hallway marble floor, and without saying a word, did something he'd wanted to do since the first day he'd met her.

He deftly disrobed her with one hand and picked up her ass with the other, pushing her firmly against the hallway wall. With his other hand, he unzipped his own pants to free the raging monster ready to burst inside and pressed his rock-hard cock against her pussy while he kissed her passionately. She was already moaning as he entered her, forceful and unabetted this time, no longer worried about his impact on her back. He rammed himself into her as she cried out in pleasure and he came in a torrent that ran down her legs and co-mingled with her own fluid.

Then he carried her onto the bed, laid her down, laughed, and said, "And how are YOU, my sweet girl? Did you miss me?" He knew he'd be ready to go again in a very short while.

Anna laughed as he wrapped her in a huge fluffy hotel towel to keep her warm. "You're amazing. I can't believe you're here! Were you planning this all along?" she said, looking at him with eyes that grabbed his heart and soul.

"Yep," Mark said, grinning, as he knew that so much of his plan still lay ahead. "You had no idea, did you?"

"None," she said, breathing his chest in as if it were pure oxygen on a mountain top. "I'm so happy."

"This is just the beginning of the surprises, baby," Mark said, looking at her beautiful face and stroking her soft cheek and voluptuous lips. "I still have many more for you. But first," he said, taking her hand and running it down to his cock that was once again hard, "I need to feel your lips there or I might just die."

"Well," Anna said, dropping the towel below her knees and showing Mark her naked loveliness, "we wouldn't want that, would we now?!" She took his engorged dick in her mouth and ran her lips slowly back and forth as she touched herself and looked up at him, and the doctor thought he'd already died and must be in heaven as he came all over her hair and face and breasts.

CHAPTER 27

NEXT STEPS

SCOFIELD REMEMBERED THINKING that no one over 50 ever had or wanted sex when he was in his twenties. But now that he was almost 60 himself, he realized that perception couldn't be further from the truth. Anna and Mark were driven insane by each other's presence, making both their drives switch into high gear, at times with no brakes at all and a seemingly bottomless gas tank.

They slept for about an hour, after which they showered together, kissing each other through the intense stream of hot water, and by the time they got out, the whole point of taking a shower had become pointless. The doctor was once more fully erect and Anna was dripping from her own reservoir.

Mark was completely overcome with pent-up animal lust for Anna, lust he'd tempered with a softer sensibility as she healed. He grabbed her hand pulling her into the bedroom and pushed her face down over the end of the bed. He saw her still-red scar line above her ass, the very line that he had cut himself and later touched that day they first kissed. It was still puffy and swollen where the huge titanium screws had been placed, and he flashed back to the terror he had felt that day in surgery, holding the power drill and praying he could get the screws positioned correctly and not paralyze her in the process.

His large hand reached down and he stroked the scar as softly as he could, knowing that was the only thing that was going to be soft about anything that was about to happen. He roughly pushed her legs apart and rammed his cock into her hot, liquid pussy that felt like fluid silk around his engorged penis.

He went as hard, but as slowly, as he could, making her moan with every thrust as he stroked the scar gently each time. Anna couldn't see his face, but he was smiling like the captain of a ship that has seen land for the first time in weeks. She cried out and he came with one final thrust and fell onto the bed on his back by her side, his hand caressing her cheek. She was crying, from pure joy, because everything he did felt amazing and right to her.

They went to sleep in each other's arms by 9 p.m., utterly and completely spent.

Anna and Mark woke up the next morning still wrapped in each other's arms and legs.

◠◡

Mark had brought the ring box with him in a small toiletry kit from his room, which Anna had no reason to search through. It was hidden underneath a tube of toothpaste, carefully closed, and covered by a few prescription bottles.

They ordered room service in bed and ate it with relish: even Anna was hungry at last. She was snuggled, of course, in his robe once more, now refreshed with his scintillating man scent, and took every opportunity to lay her head on his taut chest and breathe him in deeply.

"Just gonna go brush my teeth and then we should probably start getting ready," Mark said, jumping out of bed stark naked.

"Oh my god," Anna cried out, "Mark! We've missed our plane to L.A.! The whole crew was taking a bus at the crack of dawn and the flight left at seven!"

Even as she said it, Anna sank back onto the softly piled pillows and laughed, because she absolutely would miss a plane every day of her life to be with her beloved doctor.

"What?" Mark shouted from the bathroom with sink water running loudly as he rummaged for the ring box.

"What did you say?" He was back in the bedroom with fresh breath and dazzling white teeth and one hand behind his bare back. His shit-eating grin belied his agenda, or at least that he had one, and Anna gave him a quizzical look.

"What are you up to?" she asked him, smiling and shaking her head like we do at our dogs when they are both ridiculous and amusing. "What on earth are you up to?"

Mark hadn't really thought through his proposal word-for-word, wanting it to come from his heart in real time. He got down on one knee by the side of the bed, and looked up at Anna for the first time in his life, as he normally towered over her.

"My darling Anna," he said softly, still holding the box behind his back. "You have opened my heart and brought me a joy I didn't even know was within me. I cannot imagine my life without you now. So, with that in mind, my darling, beloved, beautiful, strong, delicate, and sexy-as-hell Anna: would you do me the great honor of becoming my wife?"

He opened the box right as he said the last few words, but Anna was still staring straight at him in stunned shock.

She crawled to the edge of the bed and looked right into his eyes.

"Yes, Mark, oh yes, I will be your wife with so much happiness in my heart, it might burst. But fortunately, you're all hooked up with the best heart surgeons in L.A., so it's all good."

He laughed heartily and took the fourth finger of her left hand, sliding the lavish ring onto her petite finger the way the prince in Cinderella slid the dirty maid's tiny foot into a glass slipper.

"It's almost as gorgeous as you are," she said, kissing him gently on the lips. He stood up to return to his alpha male status, scooped her up in his robe and carried her out onto the terrace.

"SHE SAID YES!" he bellowed so loudly that people three buildings away might have heard him but for the noisy traffic below.

CHAPTER 28

FLYING HIGH

ANNA SAT ON Mark's lap in bed, admiring her dazzling ring, and hugged him repeatedly like a child who is ecstatic about her birthday gifts.

Mark felt like a hero: to have the love of his life wrapped up in bed and having agreed to be his wife, there was little else he could want for now. He stroked her loose hair as he loved to do and hugged her gently.

"Honey, I have one more surprise for you," he said, lifting her chin towards him with one finger. "We are not going back to L.A., not yet."

Anna gave him that same quizzical look, as Mark reached under his pillow and pulled out two packets and handed them to her. She opened the folders and looked at the destination, which was dated for the next day.

"Mykonos?" she said, looking at him in disbelief. "How on earth have you been planning all this stuff behind my back with everything else going on? You're amazing… and crazy!" she said, kissing him on the mouth that she dreamed of in her sleep.

He kissed her back passionately, and throwing the plane tickets on the floor, undid her robe.

⁓

Anna and Mark arrived in Mykonos on a late September afternoon, when the weather was cool and soft breezes were coming off the Aegean. He had booked them into a five-star hotel perched high above the sea, the kind of place where air conditioning was barely necessary and the food was world-class.

From their balcony, they could see the 250-million-dollar private yachts anchored close to shore, with their tenders bringing guests back and forth to party on the exclusive beachfront.

They ate in an outdoor restaurant their first night there, and then went to the hotel's piano bar and did something they hadn't yet done in all their months together: they danced. Mark held Anna close around her waist as the pianist played slow, romantic pop tunes from decades ago. He smelled her hair and kissed it and raised her chin to look at her and realized how unbelievably happy she made him.

"Babe," he whispered in her ear, kissing it. "Let's get married while we're here. We can do it again back in the States if you want, I'd be proud to marry you twice," he said, smiling down at her. "Why don't I make all the arrangements tomorrow and you can go into town and buy a wedding dress, god knows everything is white here anyway!" he added, laughing.

It was true: almost all the bricks and cement in Mykonos were whitewashed to keep the houses and hotels cooler. Anna couldn't say no to such a delicious proposition. Since she had no family and no close friends anyway, it wasn't like anyone key would be missing.

"Yes," she said, looking up at him. "That sounds perfectly perfect, just like you."

They drank and danced for hours, and fell asleep, jetlagged, before they could even make love that night. But they made up for it in the morning before ordering coffee and breakfast on the balcony.

~

Anna took a cab from the hotel into the main shopping area in Mykonos, where hot pink and purple bougainvillea and uneven earth-colored cobblestones were the only break from the white architecture. The stores were lined up along the windy hills and narrow streets on which cabs, cars and motorcycles treacherously passed one another. Anna had gotten the name of a few boutiques to search for vintage and untraditional white dresses, and was excited to try them on.

She realized how alone she was in the world except for Mark, with no mother who would ever had helped her on such a mission, no matter what age she had gotten married. Anna didn't even have a true girlfriend to share her joy with, and it made her a bit sad, even as she came across a Pomeranian sitting on a shop owner's lap and started petting it.

She texted Mark—who was making arrangements for their wedding in a few days—and said simply, "I love you more than I can ever say. Thank you for saving my life in every way I can think of."

Scofield received the text just as he was negotiating an exquisite location near an organic vineyard on the other side of the island that he'd seen online. It was a 45-minute cab ride to get there, but he knew Anna would love the bountiful roses, the sweet animals—from donkeys and goats to roosters—who were used to run the farm organically, and the pastoral vistas.

The text made him well up, and he wrote her back: "Babe,

you are my everything, my heart and my soul. I love you with all I have in me."

He sent it, knowing it would touch her heart. They had talked about her lack of family and friends, and truthfully, while he knew it would be healthy for her to have a wider circle to socialize with, he also loved to be needed in such a god-like way by a woman so exquisite it made his heart melt.

Anna wiped away tears reading his text and continued walking the streets. She felt incredibly lucky to have found this man so late in her life, and wanted to look like an angel for him at their nuptials.

She walked into a spacious dress shop with high-end hand-crocheted white dresses everywhere and started combing through the merchandise. She knew there'd likely be no time for alterations, and had to find a size two that hugged her in all the right places and didn't need any hemming.

The actress pulled a few choices off the racks and went into a dressing room. When she came back out, barefoot, with her hair pulled up—in an airy vintage gown with a delicate white lace overlay that perfectly framed her petite body—everyone in the shop stopped what they were doing to come over and look at her.

Anna's star may have faded a bit over the past decade, but she still had a long history in the business and people recognized her wherever she went, something that still amused and amazed Mark.

"Anna Porter!" a 50-something American woman shopping in the store cried out. Two of her friends turned to look and joined in the chorus. "Oh my god!" one shrieked, digging for a small notebook from her purse. "Would you sign this for me and can we get a picture?"

"Sure, but let me change," Anna said, quickly circling back

to the dressing room to get into her jeans and cotton blouse. All she needed was someone to post a picture of her in a wedding dress on Instagram with the Mykonos dateline, and the paparazzi would be helicoptering and ruining the most precious and amazing day of her life.

⁓

Scofield—always good at masterminding a project with precision after his decades as a surgeon analyzing how to fix the most complex problems—was in his element arranging the wedding ceremony. As it would be Anna's first, and knowing that she was feeling the lack of friends or family more intensely than ever, he wanted to make sure she felt the forever-ness of their union, and his vow to be her husband, her lover, and her rock.

He made a few calls and found a magistrate who could come out to the vineyard on a Friday at 2 o'clock to perform the ceremony in English. Then he lined up a small quartet to play violin, cello, flute and harp, and a florist to cover the ceremony area in white rose petals. There would be no guests per se, so the vineyard owners had agreed to be witnesses.

Mark bought a wheat-colored linen suit, which he decided to wear shirtless with the jacket partially unbuttoned, because he knew his chest was Anna's favorite body part—or at least one of them. He lined up a hair and makeup crew for his bride to come to the hotel, and a white limo to take them to the vineyard.

Finally, he went into town and bought Anna a platinum-and-diamond baguette band to go with her lavish engagement ring, and a plain thicker platinum band for himself. He also bought her a delicate necklace to surprise her with on their wedding morning.

Anna had purchased the gossamer gown, and was on a

hunt for the right shoes and something for her hair. She didn't want a veil, but thought a jeweled hair comb would be perfect, especially if she wore her hair half up and half down.

The actress found what she was looking for after walking up several more hilly and cobbled streets, and then went looking for shoes.

Six hours later, Anna returned to the hotel to find a handwritten note on their bed and the window open with an Aegean breeze blowing the gauzy curtains in. She put down her packages and opened the heavy, cream-colored envelope and pulled out the matching card, which had script on both sides.

"Anna, my darling," it read, "if you found your outfit today, you need do no more: I have arranged for everything else," Scofield had written. "Your beauty has me tangled up in a knot of desire so intense that I cannot wait to be with you again. I'm having a cocktail at the hotel bar overlooking the sea, come find me when you get back, Your Soon-to-Be Husband, Mark."

He added x's and o's after his name.

Anna smiled and sighed reading the missive, realizing he always said and did exactly right thing to make her feel treasured, something she had never even come close to experiencing from any person of either sex in her entire life, let alone a man she was involved with.

She hid her wedding outfit at the back of the closet and changed into a breezy cotton dress and sandals and pulled her hair up loosely with tendrils in the way that she knew drove Mark wild with desire.

She found him at the bar sipping Scotch and laughing with the young Greek bartender, and sat down next to Mark with just a smile, the way two strangers do who instantly know they will sleep together before the night is done.

"May I buy you a drink?" Mark said, loving the fantasy of

having this gorgeous stranger sidle up to him. "Ginger ale, perhaps?" He knew she wouldn't touch alcohol by now, and never tried to convince her to taste it, except on his lips and tongue.

Anna smiled slyly back at him and nodded without speaking, while she reached over and took his hand and brought it to her mouth, gently kissing it while looking at him with those eyes that owned him at a glance.

"Perhaps we will bring this back to our room, Alessandro," Mark said, winking at the bartender, who smiled back at him. The young man didn't recognize the movie star, being 23 if a day, but he knew a beautiful woman when he saw one, and didn't have to be too smart to know the agenda, if not the back story that went with it.

As far as he knew, they were just two good-looking strangers on holiday who wanted to hook up, noting to himself that he wouldn't have kicked the woman out of bed either, if the opportunity ever arose.

Mark pulled out Anna's chair, grabbed both drinks, and walked behind her back to the room, watching the outline of her perfect ass move beneath her sheer dress and imagining what he was about to do to her.

CHAPTER 29

MAKING IT LEGAL

WHATEVER TRADITION DICTATED about a bride and groom not spending the night together before their nuptials, Anna and Mark had totally ignored. In fact, they had consumed each other twice before falling asleep on their last night as single lovers.

Scofield—used to waking up early after so many decades in surgery—opened his eyes first, and watched Anna sleep, her even, quiet breathing making her delicate exposed breasts rise up and down, as her hair draped all over the pillows. He reached out to ever-so-gently caress that hair and then ran his fingers equally lightly over her pouty lips, which made her open her eyes and smile at him. She moved in close to him and wrapped her arms around his neck, his aroma feeding her as if it were oxygen itself.

She wrapped her long legs around his and felt his manhood rising and sighed, still half asleep. He pulled one of her slender legs up with his strong hand and thrust himself inside her silky haven, kissing her passionately and grabbing her hair.

He poured himself out inside of her, and she came right after, and they then slept another hour before realizing they had a wedding to get ready for.

After a shower, Mark took his suit and dress shoes in a hanging bag, and grabbed the ring boxes and his surprise box as well. Scofield gave her a quick kiss on the forehead, told her he would get coffee in the hotel lobby, and that he had a special crew coming to the room for her after her shower and to text him when she was ready for it.

Anna's shower was quick, and she texted Mark as instructed, only to find the makeup and hair ladies at her door moments later. After so many years making movies and attending red carpet events, the actress knew what looked best on her, and relished the idea of having stylists there to get her ready in the way she was used to for major events.

She was relieved they spoke decent English, and told them the look she wanted.

"Very light makeup, and soft, romantic, flowing hair, please," Anna said, bringing out the large jeweled comb that would sit in the back and wrap partly around the side.

With her flawless complexion and luxuriant tresses, Anna was easy to make beautiful without too much effort. She only knew the wedding was to be outdoors and nothing else. It was a slightly overcast day, but didn't look like rain, much to her relief, although Mark had arranged for a canopy regardless to keep the potential for blistering sun at bay as much as the possibility of showers.

Anna took her garment bag and shoes and had the ladies carry them to the lobby for her. Mark was sipping coffee and looking out over the sea and smiled irascibly when he turned and saw his almost-wife, struck every time she appeared with her impossible loveliness.

He asked the ladies to put both their bags in the waiting limo and to give them a moment, while beckoning Anna over with one finger. She cocked her head, knowing he was up to something, and swept towards him smiling.

Mark reached into his jeans pocket and pulled out a box, and told her to turn around and lift up her hair as he closed a delicate platinum chain around her neck with a perfect one-carat pear-shaped diamond on it.

When she turned around, he led her to a lobby mirror so she could see it around her slim neck and then handed her a small card he had written.

"I cannot imagine kissing any neck but yours ever again, so here is something to adorn it on our magical wedding day," the card said simply, and it was signed "Love Forever, Your Husband, Mark."

Anna fought back tears. She had never imagined a day like this would ever happen for her some fifty years ago when she arrived in Hollywood, penniless and alone. But actresses do not like to mess up a good makeup job before an event, so she sucked in a breath, blew him a kiss, and said, "We better get in the limo before we miss our own damned wedding, love!"

❦

It was a long and winding drive to the vineyard, taking them to the top of the island where they could survey the Aegean like royalty, from Mykonos' highest point. The musicians were already in place when they arrived and the white rose petals—many hundreds of them—were strewn to create a floral blanket over the grassy entrance to the vineyard.

The wife of the vineyard owner helped Anna to their house to change, while Mark followed the male owner to the other side to do the same. He came out first, and stood on the white petals as the music started playing something classical, making the donkey bray and a rooster crow as well.

Anna—in her billowy sheer white lace dress that fell just below her knees—walked towards him carrying perfectly wrapped pink roses, just a few of them, with baby's breath, her hair a tumble of soft curls cascading from the comb and piled above it. Mark thought to himself that had he entered an actual castle, he could not have found a princess more beautiful than the woman walking towards him with that smile that could melt glaciers.

The magistrate kept the ceremony short, given the lack of guests. Scofield slid the tiny baguette ring on her finger as he said his vows, and looked into her eyes as if they were pools in which he could happily swim forever. Anna put the larger platinum ring on Mark as well, tearing up as she promised her heart to him.

The musicians played softly as the couple walked into the vineyard for photos and to pet the animals, kept nearby in clean stalls, and fed them apples cut up by the owners earlier. Mark picked Anna up and swirled her around, unable to believe this woman whose back he had sliced open for a surgical fix less than six months earlier was now to be his wife.

CHAPTER 30

COMING HOME

ANNA AND MARK came back to L.A. three days after their wedding, exhausted, but ready to start their lives together as husband and wife. Scofield had to focus on finalizing the sale of his share of the neurosurgery practice, which involved signing numerous documents after having his attorney comb through them meticulously.

Anna had no immediate offers for film work lined up by her agent Josh Klein, although a few of the commercial ventures looked promising. She'd decided now was the time to make a last serious burst of real money, after which, she would likely leave the business and just focus on being Mrs. Anna Scofield full-time.

She was comfortable living at the doctor's lavish Santa Monica spread now, where she felt safer. Mark loved coming home to his new wife, and she loved being there for him when he did.

Roger Niles, meanwhile, had laid low in London for more than six months. Things were not going well for him across the pond. Without the steady hum of young actresses for him to torture into shape, he felt lost, and his dependence on steroids—already well underway before the assault on Anna—started to skyrocket. His penchant for coke also escalated, although he could no longer afford the good stuff he'd been used to at the exclusive Malibu enclaves where he'd partied for years.

Instead, he had moved down to meth or crack—whichever was more readily available when he needed a fix—and it had not done much for his once-enviable appearance. But despite his physical deterioration and what effect it was having on his career, Niles was itching to return to California, where he felt sure everything would fall back together.

London may have had socialites, but they weren't as motivated as Hollywood actresses to take any amount of physical punishment to be in amazing shape, and tended to scoff at him when he tried his old technique of insulting them.

They had money and power and social standing, and he had nothing. And they were not about to be debased by some East End ruffian who'd been out of the country for two decades. Whatever reputation Roger had had before he left the UK was long gone, and making a living in the country of his birth was no longer an easy venture for the Brit.

Along with losing his looks, Niles had lost his ability to bed anyone, any time, anywhere. The steroids had affected both his sex drive and his once-instant hard-ons for any semi-attractive woman he encountered, making him largely useless to the divorcees and single ladies he'd once wowed. For a man whose entire sense of masculinity had largely rested on his sex appeal and prowess, it was a depressing reminder that he was on the skids.

Facing this reality—and with more than half a year having passed and no "Wanted" posters from Scotland Yard showing up anywhere—Roger decided the matter of whether or not he had sexually assaulted Anna Porter had probably blown over and been forgotten, or was at least not considered worthy of extradition. The latter, of course, was a chance he knew he would be taking in returning stateside, but it was a risk he decided to venture, nonetheless.

He arrived back at LAX late one night and got an Uber into the outskirts of Skid Row in downtown L.A., which was always littered with drug addicts, dealers, pimps, hos, and homeless teens who hadn't anticipated the hard climb that show business incurs. Plenty of impecunious adults lived there too, of course, all of them looking at least 20 years older than they actually were.

Niles' first intent was to score both steroids and crack, and he knew he'd have plenty of options for both. Taking the combination of the two drugs made him feel both unstoppable and enraged, and invariably brought up many feelings he'd stuffed down for decades from his neglected childhood. As his addictions to both substances grew, he had started to ruminate and become bitter, thinking that Anna had ruined his life and taken away everything he'd fought so hard for.

Along with his teeth rotting, his skin had developed boils, and he stopped the once-pristine maintenance of his appearance. He no longer ate well and began to look more frightening than appealing to women: the one thing he had always depended on as his source of income.

Roger knew that his first order of business after getting a good fix was to track down Anna. He had thought about it all the way over on the flight to LAX: he would kidnap her—and if she wouldn't give him $50,000 in cash—he would rape and then kill her, because he now had almost nothing to lose.

Britain's tabloids had been peppered with the news of Anna marrying a successful neurosurgeon, and remembering the day he'd brought his then-girlfriend to Scofield's office only infuriated Niles more. It was always the upper classes who got their way, he thought angrily, just like when he was growing up in London's East End.

⚬⚬

Niles knew that home ownership was public record and that he could easily track down Scofield's home address. He planned to wait till the doctor was gone and then nab Anna when she came outside alone. He realized it was a plan that could take minutes—or many hours—to carry out, but it was the only plan he had, so there it was.

With this agenda in mind, he smoked crack sitting on a filthy sidewalk on Skid Row, crawling with roaches and rats, and surrounded by other homeless addicts all smelling of urine and with bloated veins from too many self-injected rounds of heroin.

Roger thought about Anna's beautiful and peaceful Malibu home and shot himself up with more steroids before taking another hit on his crack pipe. He decided it was going to be all or nothing, and that the next day, he would find the star at her new home and nab her. She would either give him what he wanted, or no one would have her, and Scofield's life would be just as decimated as his own.

It was only fair, he decided. Revenge had been Niles' childhood go-to tactic when he was bullied, or when other kids got more attention than he did. He became adept at dreaming up endless schemes of how to make their lives miserable. It some-how leveled the playing field in his mind.

Unable to bear one more minute around the garrulous transients, Roger stood up and in his amped-up state, decided to find a flop house to stay in for the night so that he could set out the next day to capture Anna. He had only about seven hundred bucks left from the cash he'd brought over when he left California.

The effect of the drugs—and of being too close to totally broke—was that his mind didn't clearly assess things like risk, or even logic, and somehow the kidnapping of Anna was the only thing that made total sense and seemed like the perfectly correct thing to do. But first, he needed somewhere to take a shower and get the stench of urine off his body.

Niles walked two blocks and came to a motel clearly designed for 15-minute hookers and their johns.

The bored clerk told him it would be $30 for an hour, or $75 to spend the night, and Roger laid out three twenty-dollar bills, a ten and a five and grabbed the worn-down key. The room stank of body odor and beer, and he wasn't at all sure the sheets had been changed since the last customer, but in his wired state, he couldn't sleep anyway.

Niles washed himself with the brownish water that came out of the shower head with no soap, and then checked his backpack for his next hit of steroids and crack, which he knew he would need to embolden himself to kidnap Anna. It was the last he had to hold him over.

At about 4 a.m., he finally passed out, only to be awak-ened by a hard knock on the door at 7 o'clock telling him that he either needed to pay for another few hours or get out of the room.

Exhausted, Niles opened the door just an inch and assured

the morning clerk that he would be out in 10 minutes. Closing it, he then wrapped his bulging bicep tightly and gave himself a quick shot of steroids for an immediate energy kick. He grabbed his backpack and walked to the nearest car rental office half a mile away. He got an unobtrusive Chevy Impala in grey and searched his phone for the closest home improvement store, where he got a large roll of duct tape, a bag of zip ties, and a piece of chiffony red curtain fabric.

He grinned at the Hispanic checkout lady, who cringed at his half-rotted smile that had once been his calling card. Roger didn't look in the mirror much these days, and it was just as well, given how far his looks had dissipated in less than a year.

"Always repairs to do around the house and in the yard, that 'honey-do' list never ends!" he said with overly forced enthusiasm, none of which the checkout lady was buying. In L.A.—where meth and crack are ubiquitous—almost everyone recognizes the signs, from the brown and missing dental scape to the scabby pustules from scratching one's face. The woman knew this was a meth-head if ever she saw one, and just wanted him out of her sight and her checkout line as quickly as possible.

⤨

Niles got in the Impala and lit a cigarette. The car already smelled like an ashtray, and he was feeling antsy as the morning's crack hit had already started to wear off. He didn't have any more and had to stay focused on the job at hand: getting Anna into his car and making it impossible for her to either scream or escape. He suddenly realized that kidnapping someone solo wasn't quite as easy a task as the movies made it appear, but he had no option but to proceed at this point.

He turned on MapQuest and punched in Scofield's home

address. A Google Earth search further ensured he had the right place, but he made certain to park his dingy car a good three houses down, knowing that it already looked like it didn't belong in this expensive Santa Monica community.

His game plan—to the extent that he had one—was to make sure Scofield was gone, wait behind a tree or some bushes for Anna to come out, and then grab the actress, cover her mouth with pre-torn duct tape and quickly tie her tiny ankles up with zip ties so she couldn't run or scream. Then he'd bind her hands behind her back and throw her into the trunk of his car.

He realized he would have to carry her with her ankles zip-tied, but he knew she was light as a feather. He would then hold her for ransom until Scofield brought him the $50K in unmarked bills and left it somewhere close to the car. Knowing that the doctor would have called for police backup for a move like this, Niles decided he would have to hide Anna somewhere until he could grab the cash and disappear. Then he would leave a note where the cash had been as to her whereabouts. He couldn't risk using a phone, as it was easily traceable.

With his plan clear in his own mind, he walked up the street to Scofield's house with his hoodie pulled low, pretending to run like a jogger. He could only hope no one would find him suspicious with his backpack full of paraphernalia, but truthfully, many in L.A. who looked like perfection on Instagram and the red carpet were somewhat less flawlessly dressed getting their workouts in, and if anyone knew that, it was Roger Niles, who had been personal trainer to many of them himself.

When he got to within a few feet of the house, he ducked down and out of sight behind a large hedge along the side. Scofield was heading down to his attorney's office just as Niles arrived at around 9 o'clock in the morning. The Brit watched the doctor drive off in his fancy Porsche and felt envy and rage well up inside him, which further empowered him and made him feel justified about what he was about to do.

He ripped off a large piece of duct tape and let it hang from his jacket collar where it would be easy to grab. Then he pulled out two long zip ties and tucked them into the side pockets of his jacket. He walked low and slowly to the side of the garage and barely breathed till he heard the rolling door open and saw Anna about to get into her own Mercedes-Benz.

He dashed towards her, and the element of stunned surprise worked in his favor as he quickly put his hand over her mouth and pressed the large piece of duct tape across it as Anna tried to scream. He then grabbed both her ankles tightly and quickly zip-tied them together, after which he roughly grabbed the actress's wrists and did the same with the second zip-tie behind her back. Then he draped the chiffony red fabric around her neck so that it covered her mouth and fell behind her to cover her wrists, picked her up and carried her quickly back to his car.

Santa Monica was quiet at that time of day, with everyone either at work or playing tennis, golf, or working out at a gym. No one saw Roger speedily carrying Anna to his ratty-looking car.

He placed Anna roughly into the trunk of his car and pushed down the lid. He could hear her kicking, but he didn't plan to take long. He drove the car closer to Scofield's house, parked on a side street, and took out a dirty piece of paper and a pen and started writing in all capital letters:

$50K IN UNMARKED $100 BILLS. LEAVE IT BEHIND THE DUMPSTER ONE BLOCK FROM YOUR HOUSE IN A RED SUITCASE. NO COPS OR SHE DIES. ONCE I GET MY MONEY, I'LL LEAVE YOU A NOTE WHERE SHE IS.

He folded the note and stuck into the front door jam, where he knew Scofield would see it. Then he ran into the garage and pressed the button, running out just in time as the door came down. He didn't need neighbors noticing anything was amiss so soon.

Walking more calmly back to his car, Roger realized he now faced a waiting game over which he had no control. He also knew that once Scofield realized Anna was gone and that the trainer had her, it would be a massive dragnet to find him. But such were the chances he had to take to get his money.

Anna had stopped kicking by the time he returned to the car. He decided it was too risky to open the trunk in case anyone was watching, and it was a cool enough day that Anna wasn't likely to have passed out. But paranoia from drug withdrawal had started to kick in, and Roger was sure he saw law enforcement aiming guns at him every time he turned around.

⌒

Scofield's meeting with his attorneys lasted about 90 minutes. He had texted Anna during a break and it was uncharacteristic for her not to have texted him back, causing him concern. His intuition told him something was amiss and he drove home faster than he should have, making it back to the house in less than 20 minutes. As soon as he opened the garage door, he knew something bad had happened, seeing Anna's car with the driver's side door ajar.

He put his own car in park in the driveway and ran inside from the garage, missing the note stuck into the front door. Mark grabbed the gun from where he kept it locked and loaded at the back of the hallway closet under some of Anna's larger hats. He cocked it and walked slowly up the stairs, ready to fire if necessary. But after checking out every room in the house, he realized no one was home.

Growing up in Ohio, Scofield had learned to shoot as a boy with his father. Deer hunting was popular and occasionally they would also bag some feral pigs. He had long had a hard-to-get concealed carry permit from the L.A. Sheriff's office, to protect himself from possible addicts who knew that neurosurgeons wrote scrips for opioids.

There had been cases of doctors being held up, and Scofield had made his argument quite a few years back that he needed legitimate protection. Once approved, he bought a Glock.

Lately, of course—given Anna's fame and the coverage their marriage had received in the tabloids—he felt she was even more vulnerable to potential attackers, and that was without knowing that Niles was back stateside.

⁓

Scofield knew a missing person's report wouldn't go out so soon after Anna went AWOL, but called the Santa Monica substation anyway, just to make sure something was on record. Then he tucked the Glock into his waistband and went out the back door to check the entire perimeter of the house.

After coming up empty, he came around to the front, hoping to see tire tracks—or anything that might have been dropped in some kind of hurried exit. It was then that he spotted the small slip of paper in the front door and grabbed it.

As soon as he read it, he called the FBI.

⁓

Roger Niles' physical and mental state was deteriorating by the minute by the time Scofield placed his call to the Bureau. It had been spiraling downhill since his last early morning hit, and he was starting to feel hot and unable to focus. He became afraid that Anna might have died in the trunk of his rental car, but was too afraid to check. He hadn't heard a sound from the rear of the vehicle in hours.

Terrified of the British trainer and of the dark, constricted car trunk, Anna had actually gone into shock within 10 minutes of being locked into the horrible-smelling Chevy. As usual, she hadn't eaten much, and her delicate body passed out, unable to handle the onslaught of fear, stale cigarettes, and darkness that surrounded her.

She was certain that Roger would kill her now, a terror that sent her body over the top. She had dry heaves, but not enough food in her system to vomit, which may have saved her life, as at the angle at which he had shoved her in the car, she likely would have choked on her own upheaval.

Meanwhile, Niles' paranoia grew with each passing minute, as did his confusion. He couldn't remember now where he had told Scofield to leave the money and, of course, had no idea what was happening in that arena anyway. He started to shake violently, and got underneath the car to hide, in case any cop cars pulled up.

Like Anna, he hadn't eaten in at least 15 hours, and the rush from the steroid shot had long worn off. He was out of everything, including—he feared—luck.

⁂

Scofield didn't wait for the FBI or Santa Monica cops to show up to go looking for Anna. He knew her life was in danger and prayed he wouldn't be too late.

Mark drove methodically around the neighborhood looking for anything that might seem off and, within 15 minutes, spotted the grungy old Chevy Impala. Knowing that if it was Niles' car, Anna might be in it and that the trainer might be armed, the doctor knew he had best be careful. He quickly turned a corner and parked his car a block away, so as not to alarm Roger if it was indeed him inside.

One thing neurosurgeons learn is to come up with backup plans quickly if things go awry. In a line of work where life and mobility are always on the line, doctors have to devise Plan Bs on the spot and sometimes without as much information as they would like. Scofield thrived in those situations, which was why he'd become L.A.'s go-to spine fixer-upper. With the Glock cocked and held low and tightly by his side, he walked as quietly—and as close to the large trees that lined the sidewalk—as he could.

Niles was at a disadvantage under the car, starting to seize and unable to see, hear, or think clearly. He was shaking almost convulsively now, but reached into his filthy backpack for anything he could find to defend himself. He had an eight-inch switchblade that he'd packed in his checked bag from London and had thrown into the backpack, and pulled it out, popping up the long, sharp blade. Gripping it shakily, he moved out from under the car towards the sidewalk, suddenly feeling like his best move was to run.

But his legs were trembling so badly, he could barely stand. Sweat was now pouring down his face and he suddenly wasn't sure where he was anymore.

Scofield and Niles spotted each other at almost the exact same moment. The doctor was 10 feet away and on the street side of the car when he saw the Brit's dirty face covered in black asphalt residue, and the switchblade at the ready.

He held his gun tightly by his side and out of view, yelling over to Niles.

"Where is she, Roger? What have you done with Anna?" the doctor barked harshly.

"Dunno, sir," Niles said, shrugging as he wiped the copious sweat from his face. "Haven't seen her. No clue."

Mark suddenly felt a rage that he didn't even know he had in him, and rushed the trainer, pointing the gun straight at his head.

"Tell me where she is, and now, or you're going to die right here," Scofield said, sounding suddenly like his father when the young boy had been caught with porn in his bedroom. He cocked the gun, which auto-released the safety, meaning he could fire at any moment. Roger knew enough about guns to know that and dropped his switchblade.

"She's in the trunk, I swear I didn't mean to hurt her, I just need some money, man," he said, backing away. At that moment, four Metro SUVs and an unmarked FBI car pulled up and 10 men jumped out simultaneously, four of them immediately tackling Roger to the ground.

One of the other officers quickly smashed the driver's side car window out and unlocked the door, popping the trunk from the floor board. Anna was completely unconscious and Mark scooped her up, as officers cut the zip ties from her ankles and wrists.

"She needs oxygen and an IV stat," he told officers calmly, "We need to get her to UCLA immediately, can't wait for an EMT. Can we go in your car?"

One of the officers helped the doctor into his SUV, where he held Anna's limp body on his lap, stroking her hair. He was too focused to break down, or he would have. He rocked her back and forth and took her pulse, rubbing her hands to get the circulation back into them.

Once at the ER, he got her onto a gurney with oxygen and an IV. He stayed by her side, whispering to her that she would be ok and that she was safe now.

~

Niles was booked into the Santa Monica jail and charged with kidnapping, extortion, and—because of the harm caused to Anna and the threat on Scofield's life with the switchblade— attempted murder. It wouldn't have mattered if bail had been set, as the trainer had no one to bail him out anyway, but he was held without bail, because he was considered a flight risk.

~

Anna remained in intensive care for two days to make sure her homeostasis was back to normal. Scofield—who was now close to finalizing his partner buyout on the surgery practice—realized how much of his kids' lives he'd missed when he was able to spend hours with Anna in the ICU. She slept a lot and he would just sit and watch her in amazement, stroking her hair and running his fingers along her cheek and eyes and lips.

The sound of the various heart and breathing monitors was soothing to him, and as familiar to his surgeon's ear as a dishwasher's cycle is for the average Joe. He watched everything like a hawk, and wiped down Anna's face and chest with a cool cloth, carefully going around all the heart monitor suction cups.

Mark decided he needed to just stay by her side for the next stretch, as he knew there would be psychological repercussions once she physically recovered, given both her background with Niles and her childhood.

He started nosing around for shrinks who specialized in childhood trauma and incest issues, hoping he could find one who would come to the house while Anna recovered. As a surgeon, he knew that the sooner problems were addressed, the less likely they were to fester or get even worse.

By the third day, he was able to bring his wife home. He poured a bubble bath for her and lit candles all around the bathroom, carrying Anna gently into the large bear claw tub himself. As usual, seeing her slender frame naked consumed him with desire, but he knew his wife well enough by now to know that letting her show him what she wanted, and when, led to their most intense and combustible intimate encounters.

Mark washed Anna's hair and rinsed it with a pitcher of warm water, which felt so sybaritic and intense that she reached up for his hand and pulled it to her voluptuous lips. One by one, she sucked his strong fingers, slowly and sensually, as Mark put his head back and closed his eyes from the pure pleasure it brought him. He never could stay resolute in his intent not to consume Anna at any given moment, no matter how hard he tried. He slowly took off his pants and towered over the tub with his large member just above her head.

Anna slowly stood up and he held her waist to keep her steady as she stepped out of the tub and he enveloped her in a soft, thick towel. She got down on her knees and took his cock into her mouth, sucking it slowly and passionately, as he looked down at the goddess below him with a fire that he couldn't put out.

When he could not hold on anymore, he scooped up her tiny body and carried her to the bed and thrust into her eagerly waiting pussy with such intensity that she cried when she came. After he exploded inside her, he smiled and wiped away her tears, kissing her eyes and cheeks and lips. He had never known these feelings and their newness and fervor constantly over-whelmed him.

He put his arms around Anna and held her as close to his

heart as he could. She laid her ear against his pounding chest and sighed: she always felt like she was in a heavenly fortress when wrapped inside his strong arms and hands. She looked up at him, her chin resting on his chest, and mouthed "I love you," just as she had that first weekend they'd been together, when he blurted the same out to her.

Mark put his hand under her butt and pulled her face closer to his, so their eyes were looking directly into one another's. "With everything in my heart and soul, baby girl," he said, running his hand over the top of her hair and drinking in her loveliness. He pulled her lips to his and kissed her for minutes, and they fell asleep wrapped up in one another like an infinity knot with no beginning and no end.

CHAPTER 31

FACING THE PAST

ANNA AGREED TO see the psychiatrist that Mark had found on one condition: that her husband be allowed to sit in on the sessions also. She didn't want to face her demons alone, and by this time, trusted him so implicitly that she wanted not a single secret—no matter how dirty or dark— from Scofield.

Dr. Evan Benson was considered one of the best in the area of treating post-traumatic stress syndrome caused by being the victim of incest, as well as for adult children of alcoholics. He met with Anna and Mark for the first time in the garden of their Santa Monica home, and moved very gently into the actress's upbringing and what she had been repeatedly forced to endure as a helpless child with not a single adult to turn to or depend on.

⁓

The ongoing sessions with Dr. Benson were elucidating to Mark. Although Anna had been far more open with her husband about her childhood and Hollywood start than with anyone she'd ever met, she'd still left some of the details out, which he would now no longer be spared.

On hearing them, Scofield thought it was good that her family had apparently vanished into thin air. But Benson didn't think that letting the past rest in a dark abyss was actually helping Anna, telling both of them that the lack of closure was probably responsible for her ever-rising anxiety and nightmares in the wake of Nile's two attacks on the actress.

"Mark, I understand you're selling your practice, and I know Anna is, at minimum, on hiatus from her movie career at present," Benson said solemnly, as the couple sat hand-in-hand on the plush sofa opposite the therapist's massive recliner in his cozy Malibu office, where the remaining sessions took place.

"So, I'm wondering if this would be a good time for the two of you to go back to Anna's hometown together and try to face the past and get some answers about what happened to her family after she left. Unfinished business just hangs like a guillotine over our heads," Benson said, leaning forward.

"By finding out the truth and looking at the past through the different lens of the present day, we can hopefully dismantle that guillotine altogether and stop—or at least lesson—Anna's escalating anxiety issues, which are certainly understandable given her background."

Mark turned to look at her and squeezed her hand.

"Honey, are you up for this? Because I'm here for you if you are," the doctor said, looking deeply into her vulnerable eyes that were welling up with tears. He reached over to gently wipe one away as it spilled over onto her cheekbone. "Maybe we can put a nail in the coffin of your past," he said, turning back to look at Benson. "Will you be giving us guidelines of what to do, what to look for, and what to avoid?" Mark asked.

"Yes, absolutely," Benson nodded. "Anna, what do you think? You're going to have your husband by your side to help you through this. It's going to be different than what you remember to go back with a protector and a defender," the therapist said.

Anna was fully sobbing now, trying to catch her breath. "I don't know if I can go back," she said, gulping air as she wept and looking down at her lap. "I'm so terrified."

"I know you are, sweetheart, and so does Dr. Benson," Mark said, raising her chin towards him with one finger and wiping more tears away with his other hand. "That's kind of the whole point, though. To face demons who likely aren't even there anymore. Probably your parents have both died and if they haven't, they certainly can't hurt you now. It would be good to find out what happened to your brother, I think," he added, looking back to the shrink for affirmation.

"Yes, I think that would be good as well," Benson said, nodding. "But ultimately, Anna, it's your choice, of course. It's just that now you have all this emotional support and protection, and I promise you, it's going to be a very different experience."

⁓

Merced, California—where Anna had grown up—sits in the middle of the state, to the north of Fresno, south of Modesto and southeast of San Francisco.

When Anna was a child, it was a small town of, at most, 25,000 people, but extravagant coastal living prices had since driven population trends further and further inland, and she was surprised to see how much the area had grown in the many decades since she'd been back.

UC Merced—built in 2005 as part of the state university system—had attracted a younger demographic, and the once almost entirely blue-collar town now had a hipster element that had not been there in her youth. The approximately 90-minute drive to Yosemite made it a gateway tourist town as well, although Anna and Mark could find nothing more upscale than a Best Western to book for a week-long stay so that they could explore her past and see what they could unearth about her family.

People who live in places like Malibu and Santa Monica forget what real life looks like for most of America, taking multimillion-dollar homes, beachfront property, and the highest-end retail stores for granted. Merced might have hipped up in the fifty years since Anna had fled from it, but it was still no Beverly Hills.

They settled for a relatively upscale bed and breakfast in the heart of town and booked their stay, and from there, started to map out their plan. Mark had already found a local private investigator to help track Anna's family—or at least determine what had happened to them in the years since she had left.

After breakfast on their first day, they headed to the office of the P.I., located, quaintly, on Main Street. The owner was a hefty man with a belly that belied too many pancake breakfasts and barbecue picnics, and who looked to be close to 70. Harrison Salisbury extended a pudgy-fingered hand to first Mark and then Anna, who looked vaguely familiar to him, but he wasn't sure why.

The actress's connection to Merced was unknown, as she had fabricated so much of her past to anyone who asked about it. There were no streets named after her, no welcoming parades or keys to the city, or meetings with the mayor. And Anna was just fine with that reality.

Salisbury ushered them into his office and asked them to sit across from his desk. He smiled the fake smile of someone who is ready to retire, but can't afford to, and therefore must continue to be polite to clients whose demands he's grown weary of.

"How can I help you folks today?" the P.I. said, clearly noting they were L.A.-type people by their expensive clothes and general chichi aura.

"We're here to try to track my wife's family," Mark said, knowing the whole topic was painful for Anna to even mouth. "She left this town at a very young age and hasn't been back, and we'd like to find some closure as to what happened to her parents, who were both living when she left some 50 years ago, as well as a younger brother, who she never saw or heard from again. He was only a toddler when she left."

"I see," Salisbury said, taking old-school-style notes with a ballpoint pen on a huge legal pad. "And I presume you know all their names?"

"Yes," Anna piped in. "Mary and Jack Porter were my parents. My brother—who was 10 years younger than me and only three years old when I left town at 13—was Jerrod."

"Do you have any photos?" Salisbury asked, to which Anna vigorously shook her head in the negative.

"Ok, let's start with the easy stuff," the P.I. said, switching to his large and antiquated-looking desktop computer. "Do you know the birthdates for any of them?"

"I don't," Anna replied, realizing that sounded odd. Birthdays had rarely received notice in her house, for parents or kids, and at most were just occasions for her father to drink more and rape her again.

"No worries," Salisbury replied. "How old, more or less, do you think they would be if they were still alive today? Just a best guess."

Anna leaned back in her hard-backed chair and clasped

its arms tightly. She hated thinking about either of them and hadn't—not consciously anyway—in many decades. She guessed they had been young when they'd had her, most likely unplanned, and probably were in their very early 20s when she arrived in the world. That would make them—assuming they were still living—somewhere in their early-to-mid eighties now.

Salisbury started typing into his computer and pulled up obit records to start. People living in Merced in the 1960s were not generally health-conscious or well-off, and he knew instinctually that the chances they were still alive were likely low. But nothing came up in the town's paper, the Merced Sun-Star, which would have had records of their deaths, if anyone had submitted one.

"Nothing in obits," he said, peering at Anna over his glasses. "Do I know you from somewhere? You look so familiar to me," he said.

Anna and Mark exchanged slightly amused smiles.

"No, no, I don't think we've ever met," the actress replied honestly. She didn't think the old codger would connect her to movies for at least a few more days and figured she might as well enjoy some anonymity in the meanwhile.

"Hmmm," he muttered, shaking his head, annoyed that he couldn't place her. She certainly didn't look like anyone from Merced, with her tiny frame and perfectly maintained good looks. He guessed her to be in her mid-forties in his own head, because no one in Merced in their mid-sixties looked anything like Anna Scofield did.

"It's possible they are still alive, or it's possible they passed and the coroner may have a record of it, or it's possible they moved to another area and could be living or deceased," Salisbury said, looking away from his computer now. "Give me a few days to do some research and I'll see what I can find out. Do you have any other information on any of them? Employment, incarceration, anything?"

Anna told the P.I. about her father's decades at the chicken production plant, which it turned out was still operational. Perhaps they had some record of when he had last worked there, Salisbury said, taking notes.

Anna's mother had only worked small retail jobs here or there, and not for long. She recalled her mother had a sister in Iowa—the very one she had gone to see that fateful weekend when Anna subsequently hitchhiked out of town—but the actress had only met her two or three times in her youth and couldn't remember her name, let alone much else about her. She recalled she had a few cousins from this aunt, and vaguely remembered meeting them, maybe at a holiday dinner or a sporting event, but she had blocked out so much of her childhood, she wasn't sure about any of that.

All of this memory-digging had left Anna exhausted, and she told Mark and the P.I. that she had to rest. They Ubered back to the bed and breakfast and napped, after which she awoke feeling suddenly frisky next to her hunky man, who was more than happy to oblige. Seeing her happier made him think Dr. Benson had been right, that facing the demons of her past might really free her soul.

They showered together after having sex and dressed up a bit for dinner, although the standards in Merced are not quite what they are in L.A., where what one wears to a restaurant— especially if one is a recognizable show business persona—is critiqued and scrutinized on Instagram and E! as if it were a potential cure for cancer.

It was relaxing to be somewhere where no one seemed to know who Anna was, and where no one cared that she had married her neurosurgeon. She had never imagined she could come back to the town she had literally fled 50 years ago and feel relaxed and happy to be there. They walked in the cool night air after dinner and made out like teenagers, after which they went back to the B & B and got it on yet again.

They both slept the best they had in months.

CHAPTER 32

UNEARTHING THE DEAD

IT WAS TO be several days before the couple heard back from Salisbury, during which time they decided to be tourists. They went out to the Castle Air Museum to see old military aircraft, to the zoo, and to Lake Yosemite, a surprisingly real-looking man-made lake where they sat by the lapping water and made out again and held hands and realized that away from the insanity of L.A., life was simpler.

They talked about selling their mutual homes. For the first time, Scofield now thought he could happily leave Santa Monica behind, and Anna was anxious to get out of Hollywood and Malibu entirely. Mark was also ready for a quieter life with his beautiful wife by his side, and with whom he could share roaring fires and passionate love-making.

By the time Salisbury called them three days later, they were almost sorry to interrupt their reverie, as lost as they were in having no pressure and no schedule and just each other to spend time with. The P.I. had news for them, he said, and asked

Anna and Mark to meet him at his office so he could tell them what he'd discovered.

They sat opposite his massive desk and the investigator pushed several pieces of paper towards them. The first concerned Anna's much-younger brother Jerrod, who would have been 53 if he were still living. Salisbury found out that the boy had joined the Army when he was 24, having briefly worked at the same chicken production factory as their father. He'd been deployed to Saudi Arabia when the Gulf War broke out in 1990, and had been one of just a few hundred allied forces killed in what had been a resounding victory at the time against Iraq.

Jerrod had designated a woman Anna didn't know as his next-of-kin to receive his body for burial back home, and Salisbury had been able to locate that woman, who was still living in Merced. He had spoken to her and she'd indicated that she could tell Anna more about her brother, as well as her parents, if the actress wanted to meet up.

He also had the name of a cemetery in which Jerrod was buried, in case Anna wanted to visit his gravesite. Having given him next to no thought all of these years—after all, he had only been three when she left home at 13—she was suddenly gripped by this reality, and began choking up. But she decided that yes, she would visit his grave and yes, she would speak to his once-girlfriend. She took the number that the P.I. handed to her and tucked it into her purse, squeezing Mark's hand as if for life support.

He smiled softly at his brave survivor of a wife, so slight of stature and so big in courage, he thought, clasping her small hand back in his large one. He had to admit, he was curious himself to know more about her past, which had largely been a dark, murky canvas to him.

Anna and Mark called her brother's former girlfriend, Gracie, who was surprisingly cordial. Then again, Anna was a movie star, and the overweight, frumpy woman recognized her when Salisbury emailed the actress's picture to Gracie.

Gracie invited them to her house, which turned out to be more of a mobile home and a pretty ramshackle one at that. She lived alone there with her dog. Her one child fathered by Jerrod—a girl named Alice—was already in her early thirties and had long ago moved to Oregon. She didn't hear from her daughter much, Gracie said, offering black instant coffee in mugs that looked like they had been used approximately 10,000 times.

She was a grandmother now to a little boy named Jason and she had a few pictures of him, Gracie said, pulling the largely creased and faded images from an equally old wallet. She had met him once, when he was just a few months old, but hadn't seen him since, and he would now be 12.

Anna studied the picture of the boy—who appeared to be about seven in the deteriorating photo print—but she had no memory of what her brother had looked like.

"Jerrod and I met in high school," Gracie told Anna and Mark, who found himself wishing he had some hand sanitizer on him. Surgeons are hyper-aware of cleanliness, so to sit on one of the ripped recliners that looked like it had been pulled from a dumpster—and very likely had been—made his skin crawl.

But he knew this was a critical moment for Anna, so he stifled his disgust and put on a fake doctor-smile for Gracie. He had been introduced simply as a "retired doctor," and the girlfriend didn't probe any further.

"It was just the typical small-town romance, you know," she said, shrugging. "We got married right out of high school and I was knocked up in a matter of weeks with Alice. Jerrod was working with your dad in the Foster Farms plant, they was cutting up the dead chickens, you know," Gracie said matter-of-factly. "Deboning them and such."

Anna winced from the memory of her father's rank odors coming home from that environment and then getting on top of her. She turned to look at Mark like a helpless child who is about to drown and he stood up and looked at his watch.

"Let us take you out to lunch tomorrow, Gracie," he said. "It's a lot for Anna to take in," he added, guessing the girlfriend had no idea what the family history was here, and wondering if Alice had dodged a bullet by having her own father take one so young. Otherwise, the pattern might have been passed down to another generation.

"Oh, sure, okay!" Gracie said, excited. She hadn't been to a restaurant in over a decade, at least.

"We'll pick you up, nothing fancy, dress casual," Mark said, smiling and inwardly breathing a huge sigh of relief that he would never have to return to this junk pile that still seemed to have a lingering odor of butchered chickens, even though Jerrod had been dead for nearly 30 years.

He could tell Anna was going to faint if he didn't get her out of there fast. She was hyperventilating as they walked out the door and he got her out of sight of Gracie's house before he had her sit down and put her head between her legs so she didn't pass out. Once she felt some homeostasis return, he patted his lap for her to sit on and stroked her hair as she sobbed into his chest, almost convulsing with hysteria.

There is no greater feeling for any man than to know that he is indispensable to his woman. Anna gave Mark that gift, and it was genuine. She could never have gotten through that meetup without him, she realized, finally looking him in the eye and smiling the tiniest bit as he brushed hair back from her tear-stained face.

"You're amazing," he whispered, kissing her forehead gently and wiping her tears. "Most people couldn't have survived what you completely triumphed over," he added, kissing her hand and holding it by his heart. "I don't know what I did to deserve you, but you are the light of my life, Anna Scofield," he said, as he wrapped his strong arms around her slender shoulders and held her tight.

He was her life raft and her helicopter, scooping her from an ocean full of rubbish, one in which she had swam for the first decade and a half of her existence on Earth. She clung to him as if he were an oak in a typhoon: her only hope for staying alive, it seemed.

Scofield always got a bit aroused at these moments when he felt she most saw him as her shining knight. He carried her tiny frame to the car, and drove back to the B and B as quickly as he could, where he poured her a huge bubble bath and himself took a scrub-down shower as if he was about to go into the OR. He wanted every trace of that malodorous mobile home removed from his body surface. When he was done, he washed Anna's hair in the large bear-claw tub and rinsed it 10 times with a fresh pitcher of water that he kept refilling.

Then he wrapped her long hair in a huge plush towel and her body in a terry robe and carried her into their bed and pushed himself into her with all the force of his passion and lust for her and she relaxed into his strength and moaned until she came.

Making her climax was so erotic to Mark, it invariably made him come right after in a torrent of intensity. She loved feeling his fluid run down her leg afterwards and never wanted to wipe it away, as it felt like proof that he loved her so much and that he was everything to her that her father had never been.

⁓

After lunch with Gracie the next day, she asked if they wanted to see Jerrod's grave. He was buried at the San Joaquin Valley National Cemetery, about an hour southwest of Merced. Mark drove all three of them down there and the ride was starkly silent, as Gracie stared out the window at sights she hadn't seen in years, having never owned a car in her life.

Anna held Mark's hand the whole ride, looking out at things that looked vaguely familiar, but that she couldn't attach any specific memories to. Her stomach was upset from nerves at the thought of seeing something as concrete and final as her brother's grave.

At lunch, Gracie had told them about Anna and Jerrod's parents in the time she had known them. She met them when she started dating Jerrod in high school, and they were not in good shape by then, a reality which surprised Anna not at all.

Her father had injured himself badly on some of the equipment at the chicken factory when he came in drunk one day, and had retired on disability. He sat at home the entire day watching TV and drinking beer, from the minute he woke up until he passed out in his shredded and rank-smelling recliner.

Gracie said she would often come over to see Jerrod when their dad would be slumped over to one side of his recliner, as if he'd died. He and the recliner and the filthy carpet all smelled badly of urine from his wetting himself repeatedly in his many blackout states.

One day they came home, saw him slumped over—but forward this time—and thought it was odd that he could sleep even drunk that way. They found out the next morning that he had had a massive coronary and actually had been dead several hours when they encountered his literally hung-over body.

With no money for a funeral and no friends—not to mention a wife who despised him, one child long gone, and the other no fan of his—the father was taken away and incinerated in a mass cremation.

Within a year, their mother also passed away, from complications of cirrhosis of the liver. Both were barely even in their mid-40s, but lives of hard living, hard drinking, and an endless diet of spite and hate for one another will kill you just as surely as cancer.

It helped explain why Jerrod eventually joined the Army. He had no original family left, and even with a wife and baby daughter, no real reason to live. In his loveless home, he had learned nothing but how to cower or control, depending on which end of the bat he stood at, and the military's rigid systems and drill sergeants yelling at him in boot camp seemed little different than what he was already familiar with from his upbringing.

He was sent to Saudi Arabia at the start of the Gulf War. He went outside the camp one day to smoke a cigarette and was hit by a grenade thrown from a car that drove by. It blew off half his face and he bled out, spasming badly at the end, Gracie had been told by his comrades who ran to help him when they heard the blast.

It was an unkind death for a man who had never known kindness in his entire life.

Mark parked outside the cemetery and the three of them went in, Anna gripping her husband's hand as if for dear life. The entrance was a grey brick walkway lined with American flags that couldn't help but stir emotion in anyone walking along its path. Gracie knew Jerrod's gravesite. The markers were mostly simple stone slabs, depressed into the surrounding grass, with the deceased's name, rank and dates of birth and death engraved.

His marker didn't indicate that he was a father or a son, let alone a loving or loved one. His entire life, Anna thought as she looked down somberly at his stone, was summed up in the lack of anything remarkable or esteemed that the marker presented about him.

She felt that she should feel more grief than she did, but truth be told, she felt nothing for the brother she had barely known. She had vague memories of him running around in diapers, unwatched and often with excrement falling down his leg when his diapers went unchanged for days at a time.

"Rest in Peace," she whispered, and squeezed Scofield's hand as he pulled her in to his chest and hugged her. But Anna wasn't crying this time. She simply felt a huge sense of relief that she had escaped his fate, and she didn't mean his death by a grenade.

She had run as soon as she was able to from the horrors of her childhood, and it had probably saved her from a life of parallel obscurity.

‿

The next day, the Scofields left Merced and returned home to Santa Monica. Mark's sale of his piece of the surgery partnership was almost complete, with just papers to be signed in his attorney's office. Anna had told her agent she was taking a hiatus and not to kill any potential infomercial deals, but not to sign her on for any just yet, either.

She felt like a weight had been lifted from her soul, and walked along the beach with her husband feeling a sense of hope and peace she had never dared even dream of before.

They both knew it would be a new chapter in their lives and that leaving Southern California was almost inevitable now. Even if Anna decided to do some infomercials in the future, it wasn't like she couldn't just hop on a plane and come into L.A. as needed. A fresh start seemed in order, as they considered all their options.

⁓

Anna's Malibu pad had been restaged and put up for sale. Even teardown beachfront properties were going for five million, and they usually got snatched up fast. A pristine home with a private beach and a movie star's name attached to its history should go lightning-fast for $14.5 million, their agent had assured them.

Between the actress and the neurosurgeon—and with the expected sale of both their homes and his take on selling his share of the practice—along with millions both had saved through the years—they could pretty much choose to live graciously anywhere if they left Los Angeles.

The couple considered many options, combing through the internet country by country and state by state. One day, having arisen before Anna and drinking coffee on the deck above the garden, Scofield found exactly what he knew they needed. He smiled, bookmarked the page, and looked out towards the Pacific, realizing that most likely by that time the next year, it would no longer be his vista.

But just as he had never expected anyone like Anna Porter in his sightlines, he realized that a change of scenery and perspective could be the best thing for both of them. He went into the kitchen and made Anna toast and coffee and took it to her in bed, where she still lay sleeping.

Of course, by the time he touched her hair and leaned over to kiss her, what followed left the toast and coffee long cold and forgotten, sitting on the floor.

CHAPTER 33

MOVING ON

SCOFIELD LOVED SURPRISES: springing them on others, that was, but not getting any himself. Surgeons like as few unknowns as possible, having had to deal with so many, no matter how meticulously they plan ahead.

Mark woke Anna up one Sunday morning and told her to put on jeans and a plaid shirt, as they were going somewhere far from the manicured, Botox'd environs of Los Angeles and Hollywood. Historically, all of Mark's unexpected moves had been wonderful ones, so Anna smiled at him with a little mischief in her eyes.

"Are we going moose hunting? Or climbing the Himalayas?" she asked, intentionally batting her eyes like an ingenue.

Already fully dressed, Mark plopped onto the luxurious bed they shared and ran his hand through the side of her messy morning hair.

"We may be going to see our next home," he said with a wide grin, picking her up in his arms and placing her feet gently down on the white shag throw at the foot of their bed.

He smacked her ass and said, "Go take a shower and be ready to go in 90 minutes, 'cause we have private transportation picking us up and we can't be late."

Scofield had arranged for a private jet for just the two of them—at a cost of $35,000 round trip—including the flight crew's overnight hotel and per diem costs. The partnership sale had closed, along with Anna's house, and they could enjoy an indulgence now and again, he reckoned. He drove her to the Santa Monica airport and up to a Lear Jet where the stairs were in position for them to board.

Anna had, of course, been on private jets before, throughout her career. But never had she been on one hired by a man she adored like life itself. She turned his cheek towards her and gently kissed him on it.

"You are the most amazing man, Mark Scofield," she said, shaking her head.

A valet took the Porsche and they walked up to the Lear, with Scofield watching Anna in her skintight size two jeans that showed off her slender legs. He still got turned on just thinking about her, let alone watching her walk like a young colt still unsteady on its feet. Her long hair was loose and blew around her face as they boarded the plane, with the doctor standing behind her both to make sure she didn't fall and to watch her ass sway as she climbed the stairs.

Once inside, Anna saw tulips everywhere around the cabin. She turned back to him and threw her arms around his neck.

"The best day of my life up until then," he said, winking at her after they disentangled from their embrace, referring to that first weekend they had spent together when she had demanded 300 of the flowers if he wanted to see her. "I want you to know, every single day, that you're the best thing that ever happened to me, beauty," Mark said, guiding her elbow to her seat.

The Lear landed at Big Sky, a small municipal airport six miles from the town of Ennis, Montana. It was a tiny spot of fewer than 1,000 residents, which Mark thought would make for the perfect surround for them as they escaped the craziness of the past year and looked for peace and tranquility going forward.

They were met at the airport by a local real estate agent, Shirley Atkinson, who shook both of their hands as they entered the terminal. It was mid-autumn and the air already had a slight chill in it, even though it was a sunny afternoon and in the low 60s.

Mark wrapped Anna in his jacket and put his arm around her as they walked out of the tiny airport and to Shirley's waiting car. She had a few properties lined up to show them that Mark had carefully researched online.

The first one they arrived at had more than 4,500 acres of land and bordered the 287, the state's key freeway. Around it was Bureau of Land Management and state-owned land, Atkinson explained, meaning they wouldn't have any neighbors—not that with a piece of property that large, nosey neighbors would pose any kind of threat regardless, Mark noted, laughing.

It was miles and miles of huge rolling green hills—with some fenced areas to corral cattle or horses. It looked out onto mountains that had already seen some early snow on their peaks. From their vantage point, Mark and Anna could look down onto the valley below, which was nestled down beneath layer upon layer of ponderosa pine.

In the distance, herds of mule deer stood watching, and everywhere there were brooks and creeks creating a natural music as their water ran downhill.

The couple drove with Atkinson across the massive sprawl,

holding hands and looking with wonderment at all the wide-open spaces and expansive blue sky, which seemed as big as their love for one another.

The tiny cabin sitting in the middle of all that land was not, of course, habitable for two sophisticated city people used to all the creature comforts, but Atkinson assured them that for another million or so, they could build a 3,000-square-foot dream home and furnish it in their own style. The huge piece of land with more than 4,000 acres would run them close to $8 million, she said, and of course they would need ranch hands and maintenance workers to live on the grounds somewhere and tend to any animals they might decide to get.

While pushing on $10 million may sound like a fortune to most folks, to people used to seeing just over two acres of undeveloped land on the Malibu beachfront of Southern California go for three times that much with no homes on it, the land deal and cost of building a dream home sounded almost like a bargain. Between just their two homes, they would have enough to pay cash for such a deal and live like kings and queens to the end of their days.

Anna and Mark toured five other ranch properties with Atkinson over the next few hours and then went into Ennis to have dinner and spend the night in a funky little log cabin hotel with antique quilts on the beds and more stunning views of the Madison mountain range behind the lake.

Their charter plane was waiting for them in the morning after a hearty breakfast that Anna, as usual, ate just bites of, but that Mark devoured, and they flew back to Santa Monica, transported by what they had seen, and certain that this would be their next home.

CHAPTER 34

EPILOGUE

B Y DECEMBER—SOME TWO years later—life for Anna and Mark had changed dramatically. After deciding to purchase the Ennis, Montana property—the first one they had seen—it took 18 months for them to have a new home designed, built and lavishly furnished. And although they loved their new state, they couldn't quite wrap their minds around a log cabin—converting it instead to a home for the ranch hands—while breaking sacred Western code and becoming the much-discussed couple who built their version of a Hollywood mansion in the heart of their new Montana ranch.

If either of them had worried they might miss their former lives, they needn't have. Within a month of moving to the expansive estate, they wondered how they had ever tolerated the insanity of L.A.: its traffic, its endless search for parking, and the constant one-upsmanship that is inevitable in a city that centers on a business like the film industry.

Anna and Mark bought six horses and learned to ride from the ranch hands they hired. Mark was surprised at how easily he adjusted to not working after so many decades of absolute and unwavering discipline, but he reveled in being able to spend idle time with his wife and have picnics by any of the streams that populated their land.

He even got his grown kids to come out to the ranch for holidays and spent more time getting to know them than he ever had over the previous two decades.

Anna changed her wardrobe from designer dresses to jeans and cowboy boots. She started to eat a bit more, gaining five pounds, but as slender as she had always been, she simply had a few more curves on her still very petite frame.

They continued to make love with abandon: in bed, in the kitchen, by a river, or under one of the hundreds of ponderosa pines below their new manse. With no paparazzi to watch out for, Anna relished her increasing anonymity, needing no one but her beloved doctor Mark by her side to make her days and nights complete.

◇

As for Roger Niles, he was found hanging in his Santa Monica jail cell before he even came up for his deportation hearing. Some said he had been killed by his fellow prisoners, but with no one to care—and his aging mother still back in England— nobody ever tried to collect his body from the prison morgue. He was cremated, and his remains sat in a small cardboard box in the L.A. County Crematorium for several years, marked simply with his initials. In the end, he was buried along with hundreds of other unclaimed bodies in the cemetery behind the building in Boyle Heights in East L.A.

Anna and Mark read about his death in the papers before anyone from the Santa Monica police department ever contacted them. It marked the end of a nightmare that had haunted

Anna since her father raped her as a girl, and they never spoke of Niles—or her father—again.

∽☙

On New Year's Eve that year, Anna lay in her husband's oversized terry robe on a huge fluffy rug by their real fireplace that spewed embers.

It started to snow, and the former actress leaned into her husband's chest for the thousandth time, breathing in his manliness and putting her slender arms around his waist. He wrapped his strong limbs around Anna's little body and started to kiss her, and they made love throughout the night and awoke on New Year's Day still intertwined, which is how they wish to spend the rest of their lives.

And so they shall.

THE END

AUTHOR'S NOTE

I hope you enjoyed Anna and Mark's fictional journey. We would love to have you review "Cut Back to Life."
Please visit https://www.miranda-armstadt.com to sign up for our newsletter, including advance snippets and news of upcoming releases.

With gratitude,
Miranda Armstadt

Made in the USA
Middletown, DE
13 May 2023

30539509R00118